HAUNTED
DONCASTER

HAUNTED DONCASTER

Richard Bramall & Joe Collins

The History Press

We would like to dedicate this book to the good people of Doncaster, our long-suffering wives who put up with many late nights while we wrote it, and all the friends who we dragged along in the freezing cold on our ghost hunts over the years. Also, our warmest thanks and deepest respect must go to the departed souls who returned from the dead and kept us up late into the night. Without all of your help, there would be no book to write.

First published 2012

The History Press
The Mill, Brimscombe Port
Stroud, Gloucestershire, GL5 2QG
www.thehistorypress.co.uk

© Richard Bramall & Joe Collins, 2012

The right of Richard Bramall & Joe Collins
to be identified as the Authors
of this work has been asserted in accordance with the
Copyrights, Designs and Patents Act 1988.

British Library Cataloguing in Publication Data.
A catalogue record for this book is available from the British Library.

ISBN 978 0 7524 6375 9

Typesetting and origination by The History Press
Printed in Great Britain

Contents

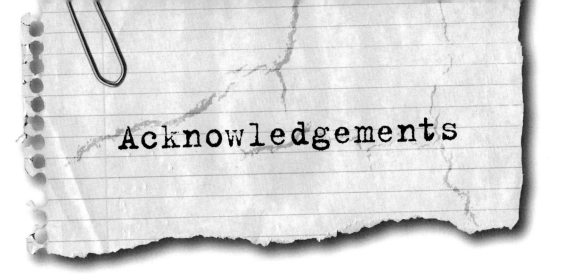

Acknowledgements

We would like to thank all of the visitors to www.rotherham-ghosts.com, who have supported us over the years and helped us create a good knowledge of hauntings throughout South Yorkshire; there are too many people to mention, but not enough thanks can be given.

We would also like to thank the former members of Dearne Valley Paranormal Investigations and Sheffield Paranormal for their help throughout this crusade.

The following people and organisations supplied us with detailed accounts of some of the events which have made the book more interesting. A big thank you to Luna Brakkan; Judy King; Tracey Ireland; Lorraine McCormack; Dan from 'The Enchanted Way'; *Sheffield Star*; *Rotherham Star*; *South Yorkshire Times*; *Dearne Valley Weekender*; *Doncaster Free Press*; The National Trust; www.Rotherhamweb. co.uk; Doncaster Archives; Conisbrough & Denaby Main Heritage Group; Conisbrough Library; Doncaster Central Library; BBC Radio Sheffield; www. the-villager.co.uk; and www.barn-burghandharlington.co.uk. Additionally, we would like to thank all of our sources who wish to remain anonymous. And finally, thanks to you, the reader, for purchasing our book; we hope you enjoy reading it as much as we did writing it.

About the Authors

From an early age, Richard encountered a number of unexplainable apparitions – some of which were terrifying. These were treated as imaginary friends by his family; despite becoming less frequent as he grew older, the sightings continued into his early teens. Consequently, he started to research reported sightings in the Doncaster area to see if others had had similar encounters. To feed his hunger to prove the existence of life after death, Richard founded www.Rotherham-ghosts.com in January 2004, where he could share information with others and see who came forward with their own reports.

Due to a traumatic paranormal experience as a child that was dismissed by parents and teachers alike, Joe felt compelled to provide evidence that what he had witnessed during this episode was not a 'dream' or his 'imagination'. This sparked his obsession with the supernatural. He read every book on the subject and searched endless websites, tracking down recorded sightings of ghosts to help him find evidence.

In a twist of fate, the pair finally met in 2006 when their obsessions with the paranormal collided. They met through a mutual friend, Gary Crompton, who was a former college classmate of Joe's and had since being working alongside Richard in a paranormal group. They soon realised that their paths had crossed many times before. Through having the same interests, they had unknowingly swapped a large amount of information through third parties and forums, and had each read and investigated the reports published by the other. They have worked together since 2006, collaborating their information to publish in this book.

Richard Bramall and Joe Collins.

Introduction

The British Isles are arguably amongst the most haunted locations in the world, and Doncaster plays its part in this. The town is widely regarded by renowned psychics as the epicentre of all negative energy; it is also home to the most covens in the UK. Over the years, we have amassed a vast amount of knowledge and experience on the reported hauntings around Doncaster – and where better to share it all than in a book, which people can refer to in years to come. Contained herein are some of the reported sightings and stories from ordinary people who believe that they have had an extraordinary experience. This book is aimed at everyone interested in the legions of phantoms that inhabit Doncaster's homes, pubs and highways.

When we ask people if they believe in ghosts, we are often greeted by one of the following replies: 'There's no such thing!', 'There's something, but I don't know what!' or 'Yes, I have seen one!' People who have witnessed ghosts, and especially those who have been involved with demonic cases, are not always quick to reveal their true beliefs. They often feel embarrassment, humiliation or even guilt.

Unfortunately, we live in a society that seems to ridicule and dismiss paranormal reports. Some large organisations do not want the public to be privy to information on hauntings at their premises. Nor do some individuals want their best friends and closest relatives to know of their experiences – sometimes going to great lengths to cover up their encounters. We are putting a number of these accounts in print, though names and locations have been changed in order to protect identities.

Richard Bramall and Joe Collins, 2012

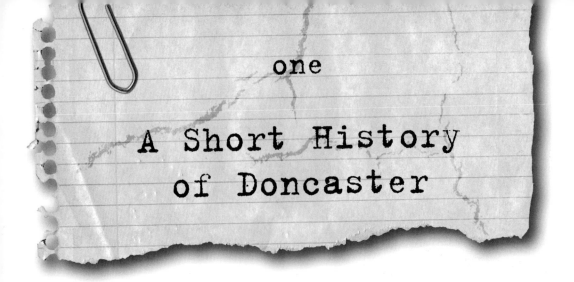

one

A Short History of Doncaster

Doncaster dates back to around AD 71, when the Romans built a fort in the area called Danum. The Saxons later invaded eastern England and called the Roman forts 'ceasters'; when they arrived in South Yorkshire, they called this fort Don-ceaster.

Around the twelfth century Doncaster was a busy little market town, but in 1204 it suffered a disastrous fire which destroyed most of its buildings. However, the town rose from the ashes and grew in size.

During the fourteenth century, friars arrived in Doncaster – unlike monks, they went out into the town and began to preach, rather than withdrawing from the world. The Franciscan friars, who came in 1307, were also known as the grey friars because of the colour of their habits.

The sixteenth and seventeenth centuries saw the little market town grow, despite various outbreaks of plague. Each time the plague struck, a considerable part of the town's population perished – but it soon recovered as more and more people moved to the area and had children.

By the eighteenth century, stagecoaches regularly passed through Doncaster, stopping at its many inns and bringing more trade and people. The railway reached Doncaster in 1849, which meant the end of the stagecoaches but brought new prosperity to the town.

Throughout the 1800s the majority of towns were dirty and unsanitary, and families lived in squalid and overcrowded conditions. Doncaster, with a population of over 10,000 people, was no different. However, by the late nineteenth century, sewers were built in Doncaster and a piped water supply was created, improving living conditions and reducing the risk of disease.

The Borough of Doncaster was eventually extended to include Hexthorpe, Wheatley and Balby. Despite being one of the main places for industry, Doncaster wasn't targeted too much during the Second World War; however, there was a serious attack in May 1941 when two parachute mines fell on the town, killing sixteen people and injuring seventy-three in Balby.

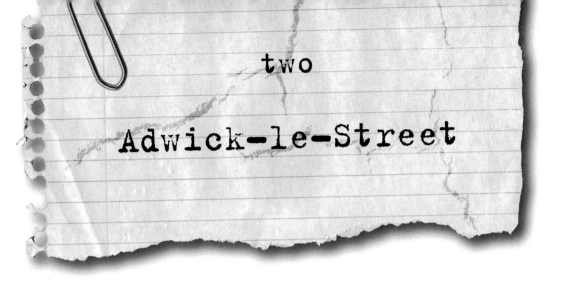

two

Adwick-le-Street

The Glamorous Highwayman

In Adwick-le-Street, a village situated a few miles to the north-west of Doncaster, there is a wood known locally as the hanging wood. A well-known highwayman named Nevison used to hide here before pouncing out on unsuspecting victims.

John (also known as William) Nevison was one of Britain's most flamboyant highwaymen – a man whose exploits and antics earned him praise from even King Charles II, who was so impressed by this gentleman-rogue that he nicknamed the highwayman 'Swift Nick'. Much about his life is shrouded in mystery, and is further confused by conflicting accounts from such writers as Macaulay and seventeenth-century pamphleteers, so it can be hard to sort fact from fiction.

It is most likely that Nevison was born at Wortley, Sheffield around 1639. He is said to have come from a good family, his father being a comfortably well-off wool merchant at Wortley Hall. However, Nevison was prone to stealing and troublemaking even at school.

He worked as a brewer's clerk in London for several years, before absconding to Holland with a debt he had been sent to collect. After a stint in Flanders, where he distinguished himself as a soldier, he returned to England and seems to have lived quietly with his father until the latter passed away, leaving him penniless – at which point he decided to take to the road and get by on highway robbery.

Nevison allegedly had a gentlemanly manner and appearance, being very charming and never resorting to violence. His romantic reputation was sealed after his renowned ride from the south of England to York in 1676, a feat later mistakenly attributed in popular legend to Dick Turpin and his horse Black Bess.

On the day in question, a traveller was robbed by John Nevison early in the morning at Gads Hill in Kent. The highwayman then made his escape on a bay mare, crossed the River Thames by ferry and galloped towards Chelmsford. He rode on to Cambridge and Huntingdon, arriving in York at sunset after a journey of more than 200 miles, a stunning achievement for both man and horse. He stabled his weary horse at a York inn, washed and changed his clothes, then strolled to a bowling green where the Lord Mayor was playing bowls.

He engaged the Lord Mayor in a conversation and then laid a bet on the outcome of the match – Nevison made sure that the Lord Mayor remembered the time the bet was laid: 8 p.m. that evening.

Later, Nevison was arrested for the robbery in Gads Hill and, in his defence, produced the Lord Mayor of York as his alibi. The court refused to believe that a man could have committed the crime in Kent and ridden to York by 8 p.m. the same day. Nevison was found not guilty of the crime but was called to present himself before the King to explain the feat. Knowing that he could not be tried for the same crime twice, Nevison was happy to boast that he had ridden as fast as Old Nick (The Devil).

There are few other accurate records of Nevison's career. His gang of six outlaws met at the Talbot Inn at Newark and robbed travellers along the Great North Road. He was arrested several times and was sentenced to transportation to Tangiers, but returned to England (or escaped before the ship disembarked from Tilbury) and once more took to highway robbery. He was arrested yet again in 1681 and escaped with the imaginative rouse of 'playing dead' – getting an accomplice to masquerade as a doctor and pronounce him dead of the plague.

The net was beginning to close in around Nevison, especially after he killed a constable who was trying to arrest him. He was soon tracked down by bounty-hunters and was hanged at York Castle on 4 May 1684. His body was buried at St Mary's Church, York, in an unmarked grave.

Since his death, his ghost has reportedly returned to the scene of better times. Adwick-le-Street woods were once, apparently, well frequented by 'Swift Nick' and many of his crimes took place there; the area is also rumoured to have been the home of his secret lover.

Today, sightings have occurred along the stretch of road near the wooded area. Motorists presume him to be a hitchhiker, but, after slowing down to help, they soon realise that this is the figure of this once notorious highwayman who still haunts the roads. He holds up his left hand in a stop motion before brandishing a flintlock pistol in his right, then fades away before their very eyes, leaving the travellers dumbfounded.

The Highwayman, named after Nevison. (Authors' collection)

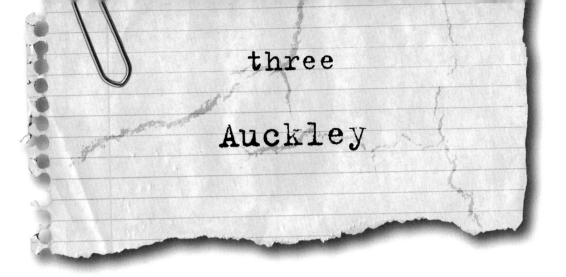

three

Auckley

Toast to the Ghost

Auckley, which lies approximately five miles from the town of Doncaster, is set in beautiful rural surroundings. However, many locals and visitors are unaware of the spooky goings-on there...

Auckley is home to a famous Grey Lady apparition, who has made appearances at the rear of crowds – particularly at weddings and christenings – for more than 300 years. The story goes that she was the youngest daughter of a local man and was kept as little more than a servant. She had little opportunity to meet a man herself and took solace in the happiness of others, so where possible she would attend joyful occasions to absorb the happiness that she longed for.

After her death, many people reported sightings of the young woman and it soon became a custom to set a place for the Grey Lady at special events and say a toast in her memory:

We wish thee joy on this our celebration.
Come sit thee down and take a glass of wine.
And if you sup in our felicitation,
The hour is blest as blessed you may be.

The Lingering Local at the Eagle & Child

That's not all that happens in this quaint village – the Eagle & Child public house, which is situated in the heart of Auckley, is rumoured to have several ghosts. The one most regularly seen by staff and locals is a man of scruffy appearance who sits at his favourite table – table 8 in today's current layout. Once he is spotted, he disappears, leaving his cigarette smoke lingering.

Local legend says that when the pub went through one of its many improvements, the landlord banned the man from coming in while wearing dirty work clothes. He apparently died the next day, the cause of which is unknown. To date he seems to have taken a fancy to one of the cleaning girls who works there and appears more to her than others.

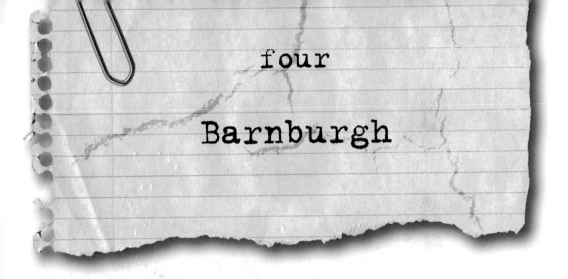

four

Barnburgh

The Cat and Man

St Peter's, Barnburgh, is known far and wide as the 'Cat and Man Church'.

In the fifteenth century, a worthy knight called Sir Percival Cresacre was returning home on horseback late one night. At that time, there were no roads and very few houses, and the land between Doncaster and Barnburgh was thick with woodland. It was a dark and lonely ride.

Somewhere on his way between the tiny settlement of High Melton and his home at Barnburgh Hall, Sir Percival was attacked by

A common depiction of a familiar. (Authors' collection)

a wild cat. This cat was no pet; it was much bigger, stronger and more dangerous, and is described as having the stature of a puma. It sprang out of the branches of a tree and landed on the back of Sir Percival's horse. The horse was so spooked by the tearing claws that it shied, sprang forward, and threw its rider to the ground before bolting away. The cat then turned upon the knight and there followed a long, deadly struggle between the two, which continued all the way from Ludwell Hill to St Peter's Church. Upon reaching the church, Sir Percival tried to gain sanctuary inside; he managed to open the first doors to the porch and tried with all his strength to shut the cat outside, but failed. Both Sir Percival and the ferocious wild cat were completely exhausted by their dreadful struggle. With his last breath, Sir Percival managed to crush the cat to death with his feet, against the wall of the porch.

Sir Percival's frightened horse had returned to the hall without him. His family and servants, fearing an accident, began a frantic torch-lit search. By the time they found Sir Percival, he was dead. The awful wounds made by the cat's razor-sharp claws had tragically killed him. To this very day, a bloodstain on the floor of St Peter's Church porch marks the scene of this gruesome story.

Running between the side of the church and rectory is a ginnel which is reputed to be haunted by the cat and man, who are still locked in battle to this day. People have often experienced feelings of foreboding and dread whilst walking along the path at various times of the day. Several dog-walkers have reported that their dogs have stopped dead in their tracks and refused to go any further down the lane, whilst snarling and barking as if there's a foe blocking their path – even though the owner can never see anything.

Around twenty years ago, a young woman was taking a shortcut through the ginnel one evening. The footpath was quite dark and a mist was forming. Not alarmed by the atmosphere she went on her way, as she had done many times before. All of a sudden, she heard what she describes as a snarl and spat from what seemed to be a very large cat. Startled, she spun around and saw what appeared to be a spherical blue light floating in the ether, slowly growing in size. She leaned forward and peered through the mist to try to focus on what the shape was – it started to manifest into the torso silhouette of a knight. Terrified at the sight before her, she fled in a state of sheer panic. Could this have been the chivalrous knight protecting her from that cat?

St Helen's Chapel

The chapel ruins lie close to what was part of the Roman Ricknield Street, now known as Hangman Stone Road. Not far away from here is Barnburgh Grange. The Grange was part of Nostell Priory and was once reportedly used as a nunnery. It is said to have housed several priest holes, along with an underground escape passage to St Helen's Chapel, for use during the time of the Dissolution.

The ghost sighting is that of a lady in a white dress and a black, hooded shawl, seen walking from the nunnery to the chapel. Her journey takes her along the route directly above the rumoured tunnel. She is believed to be the restless spirit of a nun who tried to escape the confines of the nunnery by using the secret passage. Sneaking into the tunnel after dark she became trapped, and died of asphyxiation due to lack of ventilation. It was some time before her corpse was found and now she's doomed to walk forever along the route that marks the scene of her tragic death. Motorists and walkers often report seeing the spectral figure around autumn at dusk.

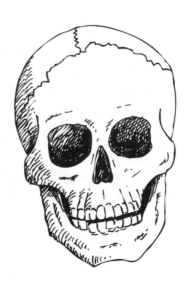

five

Bawtry

The Haunted Hotel

The Crown Hotel is a Tudor-style white building with black timberwork that stands in Bawtry Market Square. It boasts a narrow courtyard leading through to the rear, where the remains of the once well-used stables can be seen. This seventeenth-century coaching inn was once a posting house and legend has it that the infamous highwayman Dick Turpin once stayed here. People swear that the clattering of horse hooves can still sometimes be heard in the courtyard.

The Crown retains the ambience of a bygone age, a quality that is emphasised by the reputed presence of several ghosts which haunt the hotel. One spirit is that of a waitress who was murdered by her jealous lover after she rebuffed him for a more prestigious admirer. It is said that she only accepted the advance of the other suitor in a bid to make her lover jealous and force his proposal of marriage. However, after he returned late one night to reclaim his love, she still rejected him – he was drunk and she simply wouldn't believe his intentions. Furious at this, he strangled her to death. The screams of this lady are said to be heard at around midnight every year on the anniversary of her death.

Another one of the Crown's ghosts is said to be that of an elderly monk who suffered a heart attack in the old stables. People have reported smelling a strong aroma of brandy, before seeing a portly figure in brown robes sitting in the corner laughing, before fading into the brickwork.

One of the more frequently sighted ghosts reported by staff and guests is the Crinoline Lady, who is said to have perished in a fire many years ago and now walks the corridors of the old wing at night.

six

Bessacarr

Ghostly sightings at the Air Museum

The epicentre of the hauntings at Doncaster Air Museum seems to be hangar 21, which was originally constructed to accommodate 616 Fighter Squadron in 1938. Various incidents have been reported – from dark shadows, light anomalies and even poltergeist activity, including a full-bodied apparition of a pilot in the main hangar. People have also reported having their hair stroked and being touched, and scratches have appeared on their bodies when nobody is around. In addition, some individuals have been overcome with extreme sadness for no reason.

There are also reports of the ghost of a young boy named Mickey. Mickey lived in this area during the Second World War and is believed to have been sent to Doncaster during the bombing. It is not known how he died. In addition, at the end of the corridor in hangar 21 there is a book which details names, addresses and ages of people associated with the area. Staff claim that no matter what page you leave the book open on, it always goes back to the same place, which bears the following information:

OLDFIELD, MICHAEL, BRIAN. AGE 6 OF 39 BROOMHALL ST, STEPSON OF ROBERT WILD. 12th DECEMBER 1940 AT 39 BROOMHALL STREET

Several ghost-hunting groups have visited hangar 21 and have reported seeing the solid mass of a large human shape moving directly past the larger-than-normal doorway. The figure seems to be a man dressed in what they describe as a boiler suit, who walks past the open doorway straight through the handrails and disappears without a trace. Upon approaching the doorway, the investigators trip the security lights, which are on sensors – which leaves them to wonder why the figure didn't also cause the lights to turn on. What's more puzzling is that the outside area is paved with pea gravel which is loud underfoot, yet the figure makes no noise.

The investigators are left with the cold realisation that each and every one of them had indeed come within metres of an apparition.

Wailing Woods

Running along the border of Warning Tongue Lane is a twenty-hectare woodland called Black Carr Plantation. Woodland was planted to beautify the landscape, to provide timber for the estate, and so that gentlemen could enjoy the fashionable pastime of shooting wildlife.

In the eighteenth century at harvest time, a couple who owned a small holding on the outskirts of Doncaster went to market to sell their produce. They did exceptionally well considering it had been a harsh summer. They waited around until 3 o'clock for the judging of the best-bred pig, where the grand prize was a large barrel of beer. They had entered their prize sow in the competition. To their amazement, their prize pig scooped first place and made a healthy profit as the hammer fell. Happy at their windfall, it took six men to load the barrel onto the back of their empty cart. The farmer tapped the barrel and paid the men in beer, then joined in the final celebrations of the day with the rest of the farming community.

The couple, along with one of their acquaintances, did not set off on their journey home until the sun started to set. Worse for wear, they decided to continue their celebrations, frequently refilling their flagons from the tapped barrel at the back of the cart – this made their journey longer than normal and by now a thick fog was drawing in.

They got to Warning Tongue Lane when tragedy struck: drunk and unable to see where they were going in the fog, they drove the horse and trap into the ditch. The horse whinnied and the woman screamed, as the cart was now at a 45° angle and slammed into the bottom of the banking, breaking the barrel loose from its holding. The barrel rolled over the three companions and horse, killing the two men and horse instantly before catapulting the cart on top of them. The woman was now trapped underneath the carnage, barely alive, and it was only her screams that brought rescuers to the scene.

Despite working till daybreak, they were unable to free the woman and sent for a priest because they knew she wasn't going to make it. Tragically, the woman died just before he got there. Knowing that it would be difficult to retrieve their bodies, and fearing that children would see the gruesome sight, the priest sent for more men from his local parish to bury the trio and horse at the side of the road where they had fallen. He then performed a service where they lay and a small marker stone was later erected at the scene.

Today, people walking this road have reported hearing the sounds of the tragic accident replaying – the sound of an approaching horse and cart along with voices of merriment, then the strained cries of a horse, a scream of a woman, followed by a clatter as the trap goes down the banking, then the snap of a rope and rumbling is heard as the barrel breaks free, before the agonising death groans of the two men and the final whinny of the horse, ending with an almighty crash as the cart lands on top of them. All is then quiet for a few moments until the silence is broken by the excruciating wails of a woman. The cries are reported to go on for some time and can be heard echoing throughout the Black Carr Plantation. This is where it gets its name 'Wailing Woods'.

We have visited this road on a number of occasions whilst researching this book, but have been unable to track down the exact location of the accident or the stone.

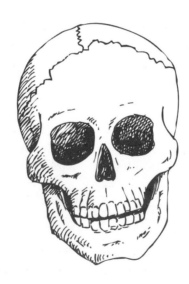

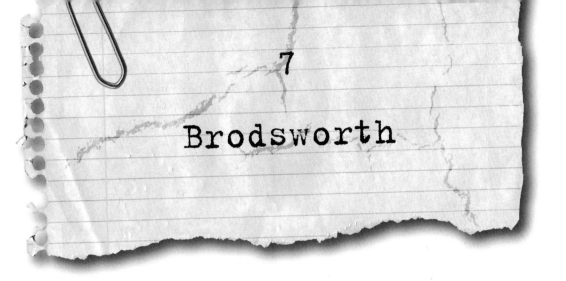

7

Brodsworth

Brodsworth Hall

Brodsworth Hall was built in the Italianate style of the 1860s by the fabulously wealthy Charles Thellusson; his descendants occupied the hall for many years. Various ghostly sightings and experiences have occurred in the building, including the dining room door handle turning on its own accord, followed by the door opening and the chairs being drawn away from the table by an invisible force. A man wearing a tweed suit has been seen sitting in a chair at the grand table; he is thought to be the ghost of the late Augustus Thellusson. Witnesses have described the same man sitting at the table smoking; he turns his head and smiles in acknowledgement of their presence, before disappearing.

Augustus isn't the only ghost to haunt the grand house; a lady in Victorian dress has been seen descending the staircase, disappearing as she reaches the foot of the stairs. There have also been sightings of a man who is described as wearing a khaki uniform, possibly from the era of the First World War, who appears at the top of the staircase, startling unsuspecting people as they ascend. He stares coldly into their eyes before turning on his heels and drifting into the adjacent room, where no trace of him can be found.

Female members of staff have reported an unruly ghost in one of the upstairs rooms. After entering the room, they are pushed in the back, as if being ushered out by a pair of invisible phantom hands. Because of the unknown force, some of the staff now refuse to enter the room.

Over thirty years ago, a courting couple were outside the gates of Brodsworth Hall when all of a sudden a mist started to appear in the shape of a man from the waist up, wearing what appeared to be a three-cornered hat. The couple were quite scared at this and sped off. Looking into the history of the site, they found that the place where they were parked used to be part of the old Great North Road, and many others had also witnessed a strange fog forming into the silhouette of a man. Could this be linked to the Swift Nick sightings at Adwick-le-Street? Or the knight's silhouette at Barnburgh?

Brodsworth Hall as it stands today. (Authors' collection)

The church where the ladies disappeared. (Authors' collection)

St Michael's Church

One evening, a young couple walking through the churchyard spotted two elderly ladies, in clothing from a bygone era, walking towards them along the same path. The young couple stepped into the church porch to allow them to pass, and, while waiting, listened to the footsteps and chatter of the two old ladies – but the sounds cut dead mid-stride, leaving an eerie silence. Wondering why the noises had stopped, the couple stepped out of the porch and scanned the graveyard for the two old ladies – who had simply vanished without a trace.

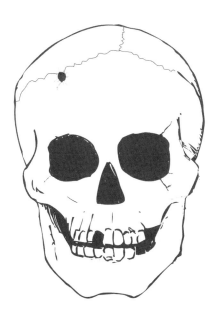

Burghwallis Hall of Horrors

In contrast with most of the villages surrounding Doncaster, Burghwallis had very little suburban development during the nineteenth and twentieth centuries. Today, the village has retained much of its original character and has a feeling of peace and tranquillity.

Burghwallis Hall is also known as St Anne's Convent. Originally there was a chapel in the attic – until 1797, when Michael Tasburgh-Anne built the southwest chapel wing, rendering the original chapel forgotten and obsolete. Like most chapels of that time, the original was built with a priest's hiding-hole that was secretly accessible from the chapel, and was only discovered in 1908.

The house was later changed into a rest home for the elderly. Then in 1986 it was sold to the Dominican Sisters of Oakford, a South African Foundation who had extensive structural and internal works done, including building a new chapel. Today, the site continues to be a rest home for elderly ladies and a Chapel of Ease for Blessed English Martyrs. The mansion is now known as St Anne's Rest Home.

It is rumoured that, on 14 March 1934, a mother smothered her son while he slept; she then concealed the lifeless body in a closet in one of the upstairs rooms. Later, her husband discovered the body and, horrified at what his wife had done, he murdered her in a homicidal rage before taking his own life in despair. Since that fateful night there have been reports of an old music box still heard chiming through the corridors of the old building; this is normally followed by the voice of a small boy singing along to the melody.

Despite one owner's adamant denial that Burghwallis Hall is haunted, subsequent occupants have seen numerous spectres of men, women and children from the other side. Another heir to the mansion, Major George Anne, is said to have been woken by a ghost while he lived at the hall during the last war. He claimed that the apparition of a thin old man with a greenish hue, had pulled the bed mattress up and down violently whilst staring at the Major with an expression of hatred and loathing. The Major believed it to be his great grandfather, Michael Tasburgh, who may have known of his plans to sell the hall.

In addition to this, a small woman dressed in dark clothing and a black hat is seen gliding her way down the corridors, illuminating her way by dim candlelight and terrifying guests and visitors alike.

Other witnesses claim to have seen a man dressed in grey dashing down the staircase before dissolving into the ether. The same figure is reported to have woken up one woman resident who was staying there. She described him as having a look of lunacy and rage. He stood over her bed before leaning over and staring at her face, then vanished as she hit the light switch.

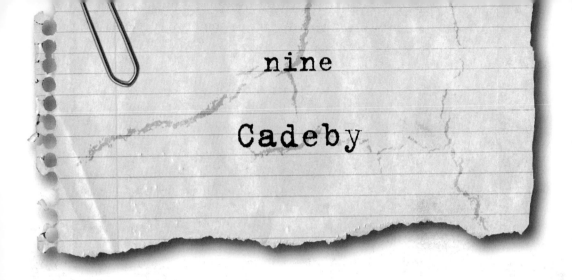

nine

Cadeby

Cadeby Pit Disaster

Early in the morning of 9 July 1912, an explosion took place in the south-west portion of the Cadeby Main Pit and, of the thirty-two men at work, only two survived. A rescue party of fifty-three men was sent below to look for any survivors and the task of bringing the bodies to the surface began shortly after 9 a.m., by

The original team who would have helped search for survivors in the pit disaster. (Authors' collection)

The old pit head that stood near the train crossing at Denaby. (Authors' collection)

which time it was estimated that between twenty and thirty men had perished. The work of the rescue parties was seriously hampered by the heavy falls – then another large explosion, followed by a series of smaller explosions, took place, resulting in a death toll that was more than double that of the original disaster.

The noise of the second explosion was heard two miles away. Other rescue parties were summoned to help and crowds gathered in the pit yard as anxious relatives waited for news. It was announced in the evening that seventy-four were known to be dead and it was feared that the total would eventually be higher.

The total loss of life was eighty-eight men, including three inspectors of mines, and the managers of both Cadeby and nearby Denaby Main Colliery. The death toll could have been much greater had it

not been for the fact that most miners had taken the day off to witness the visit of King George V and Queen Mary at nearby Conisbrough Castle. There were only 111 men at work on the day of the explosion; on the same shift the week before there had been 489 men.

In 1955, a miner from Denaby, named Jack Clarke, was working as a deputy at Cadeby Pit; he arrived for his shift as normal one winter's morning, before the main shift started. Pit deputies held a position of high responsibility and were accountable for the safety of men underground. Jack was checking pit props, which support the roof, and ensuring there was no subsidence. It was common practice for Jack to go down alone and check coal seams before the shift started.

Jack was a stickler for routine and always started at the furthest point then worked

Standing up to look where the voice was coming from, he called back, 'Who is it? What do you want?'

The voice replied in an urgent tone, shouting, 'Come here, I need you.'

Leaving his snap box and belongings behind, Jack headed off down the tunnel, following the voice and thinking that someone wanted his assistance. As he travelled, the voice continued to call, 'Jack, come here, come this way.' This seemed strange to Jack as the voice seemed to be moving further away from him.

Then he was distracted by the sound of a rumbling noise coming from behind, followed by a gust of wind and coal dust blowing past him. He ran towards the voice that was calling him. However, after searching he couldn't find anyone and the voice had stopped shouting. Heading back towards the area where he had been sitting, he was shocked to discover that the ceiling had collapsed, burying his snap box under a pile of rocks and coal. A cold shiver ran down his spine as he could easily have been killed.

Jack said on numerous occasions afterwards that he believed a ghost had saved his life. Could this have been one of the rescue crew who had died years earlier during the disaster?

his way back towards the main entrance. On this day he did just that. As he got near the head of the shaft, he had about half an hour to spare before the main shift started. So, he sat down against the wall, opened up his snap box and tucked into a sandwich. He was sat there for around five minutes when he heard a voice call out, 'Clarkey!' He was slightly confused as he'd thought he was the only one there. Then the voice called again, 'Jack, Jack! Come here.'

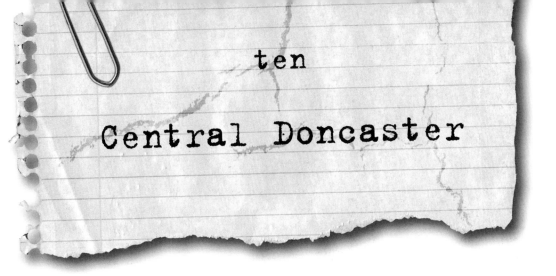

ten

Central Doncaster

Free Press Offices

The free press offices in Doncaster were built in 1925 and are reported to house a number of ghosts. These include an old insurance clerk, an Eastern European debt-ridden tailor, and a murderous boxer who lurks in the basement. But the grizzliest tale is that of a man who apparently sent his teenage sister to work as a prostitute in the town. She wanted to stop and he murdered her in a fit of rage. Overcome with shame and remorse, he took his own life on the railway lines near North Bridge and is said to haunt the press offices today.

In addition to this, staff have reported dark, ghostly shadows, spine-tingling unexplainable drops in temperature, and disembodied footsteps tapping along corridors in the twilight hours.

The Mansion House

Doncaster's well-designed eighteenth-century Mansion House has always been a focus for civic pride and has dominated the High Street for over 250 years. It is one of

The grand house as it stands today in central Doncaster. (Authors' collection)

only four surviving civic Mansion Houses in the country.

The Mansion House is reputed to play host to a mischievous phantom who was a former mayor's attendant. The ghost is described as tall with a military bearing and has even appeared in group photographs. He has allegedly also opened car doors, joined in processions and admired paintings of members of the royal family, particularly the full-length portrait of Queen Victoria.

Regent Square

The following story was sent to us by a lady called Luna. She has asked us to keep the exact location secret, but we can tell you that the incident happened in Regent Square, Doncaster in the late 1990s.

Luna was a young student looking for a new home. Her friend Aidy lived in a downstairs flat and she decided to stay there one night. Their friend Andy lived upstairs. Aidy's flat was in the former servants' quarters of a once grand house, a lot like the mansions portrayed in *Oliver Twist*. It was built in 1882 and is a Grade II listed building.

Luna loved the grand old house and it seemed like fate had smiled on her when a well-spoken gentleman came that night to collect the rent and offered Luna the tenancy on the flat next door. It was like it was meant to be. She was so excited at the thought that she soon moved in – taking with her a number of small pets that included hamsters, chinchillas and guinea pigs.

During Luna's first week in the flat, a strange old woman who lived on the top floor befriended her and said that the building was plagued with dark entities. Luna thought that she was just an odd character and didn't pay much attention. However, within a few weeks the woman moved out and took with her every trace of her existence – even down to the paint on her front door, which she had spent her last few days sanding off. She explained that she didn't want to take any of the dark energy with her.

Not long after moving in, Luna started to feel uneasy. This resulted in her sleeping on the sofa in the lounge with the television switched on – but even then she couldn't shake the creepy feeling that she wasn't alone.

After several weeks, things started to take a turn for the worse – light bulbs started to pop and there were major problems with the electrics, causing power dips and complete power failures that only seemed to be affecting her flat. She also started to hear someone calling her name late at night and a baby could often be heard crying, even though there were no children in the building. Other phenomena followed, including the sound of a bell that chimed intermittently throughout the night.

One evening, she heard footsteps in her flat which seemed to be heading towards her bedroom door. She was home alone with the doors locked and her heart started to pound. Luna thought that an intruder was approaching her room; the footsteps stopped and there was a loud knock on her bedroom door. At that instant, the lights went out and the phone began to ring. Luna went to grab the phone but it fell from its stand to the floor; she frantically grabbed it and started to cry for help, but all she could hear on the line was white noise crackling. Then, all of a sudden, the lights came back on and the dial tone returned. She screamed for Aidy, who came round and found her in a state of distress – he'd not heard anything from next door and hadn't lost any power either.

Luna was now scared to be in the flat alone and asked a friend to stay with her. Things became more sinister when the electricity went out again. This time it was different to before – Luna said that she could feel something evil lurking in the shadows; it got so bad that Luna and her friend left the house in the middle of the night and walked the streets until morning, too scared to stay there.

They ventured back to the flat at daybreak and could see from the street that the lights were back on. They slowly entered the flat and looked around to see if anything was amiss. Luna checked on her animals and was horrified to see that one of her chinchillas had chewed its own leg off right down to the bone. Her friend dashed to the hamsters only to discover that both were dead in their cage, one with its eyes popped and the other with its stomach slit wide open. Distressed and wanting to know what had happened to them, she took them to a vet, who said that the hamster had been dissected with surgical precision and the death was not natural.

Luna was left not knowing what to do as she couldn't afford to move. At the end of her tether and frightened, a friend eventually suggested that she seek help from a local medium. He came to the flat and seemed to know instantly what the problems were and said that he'd do an emergency clearance.

She waited anxiously upstairs in her friend's flat. The friend had also endured some strange experiences. Things had turned up in the fridge that she had lost the day before, footsteps moved around the flat and she had suffered an oppressive feeling, but the most traumatic experience was an axe turning up in her bed – her friend described it as being like something out of a horror movie.

The medium started by setting up two white twelve-hour candles, which he left burning in her bedroom to rid it of evil; he felt that that was where the hub of activity was. He told Luna to leave them burning and under no circumstances to put them out. Luna and her friend decided to go out for the evening and let the candles do their work. She was feeling happy at the thought that someone believed her and that her problems might be coming to an end.

They returned home later and went to check on the candles; all seemed well until Luna opened the bedroom door. Luna described the room as looking like a bloodbath: only the candlesticks were left, the white candles had turned blood-red and exploded all over the room, leaving red wax dripping off all surfaces and walls. Luna was shocked, speechless and crying, but most of all wondering how the candles could have turned red.

She called her neighbours, who all came round and helped clear up the carnage. It was then that her neighbour told her that a friend had seen a twisted, hunched figure in the window of her flat, whilst she was at work.

One night, Luna had some friends around for a drink; the final guest to leave was Andy, who lived upstairs. All was quiet until she was startled by a frantic knocking on her front door. She ran over to answer it only to find Andy as white as a sheet and clearly in a state of shock. All she could get out of him was 'Come and look', so she followed him to his flat. Shaking, Andy took Luna to the bathroom. She could see that the toilet bowl was smashed to pieces – not only that, but everything that was on the shelves had been swiped off and was scattered about. The sink and bath taps had also been turned on and were running at full force.

Andy confessed that there had been lots of other things going on too, but he had been too scared to tell anyone for fear of ridicule. He said that on more than one occasion, normally when his girlfriend was staying over, they had been woken to see a young blonde girl in a 1940s' red coat standing at the bottom of their bed. He said that she just stood there staring at them before walking to the wall and disappearing. Also, they had both experienced hearing the footsteps and voices calling their names.

About a week later, Andy and his girl-friend arrived home, climbed the stairs and reached the flat door. As they entered the threshold arm-in-arm, an unknown force hurled them both to the floor and slammed the door shut in their face.

After this, Luna knew that she had to take some drastic action and took a spiritual awareness course in a bid to understand what was going on in the house. She needed to have closure and was sick of living in fear. She asked her friends and neighbours to join her in a séance, but they failed to contact whatever was there.

Luna's boyfriend Paul eventually moved into her flat, after spending a year or so living in one of the upstairs flats. In his time there he had also been plagued by the footsteps, electric problems and voices, and had suffered mysterious bruising around his wrists and throat. The worst for him was an event that took place one night when he was half asleep. He described seeing a shadow come down into his room, which pinned him violently to the bed and rendered him paralysed; this had started to become a frequent occurrence until he moved in with Luna.

Things became more frightening for Luna in the latter part of her time at Regent Square. One night, whilst home alone, she climbed into bed and noticed that it was wet. Getting back out and turning the light on, she pulled back her duvet to reveal a dark silhouette of herself in putrid water. It was like someone had lifted up her duvet and carefully drawn her outline before putting the duvet back. This terrified her as it had singled her out for a personal attack.

Luna's final experience was her scariest and she describes it as a type of sleep paralysis – but it was so very real. It was a normal night and she'd gone to bed about 11.45 p.m., after staying up talking to a friend who was staying the night on the sofa in the front room. Her boyfriend Paul was already in bed asleep. She climbed slowly into the bed, not wanting to wake him, and lay there in the dark. She could hear some type of whispering that seemed to be coming from outside the window. Thinking it was someone in the street, she strained her ears to try to identify who it could be, but the words were too faint to understand.

Suddenly she came over feeling quite sick; the voices began to escalate into a hungered chatter, all talking over each other, making the words inaudible. Looking around the room to see what the noise was, she saw the same dark entity that Paul had described appear in the corner of the room. It made its way forward and hovered above their bed; Luna's pulse was racing and she was feeling sicker by the second. She went to get up to clear her head, and it was only then that she realised she couldn't move – she was glued to the bed and could feel a pressure bearing down on her, as if a large person was lying on top of her.

Although she was fully aware of her surroundings, a vision was beginning to play in her head like a movie. It was like information was being poured in, but too much for her to take in all at once. The visions began in a first-person view of standing behind an unbolted door, yet at the same time she was fully aware of being in her own room in bed and could even hear the TV in the lounge playing. She was looking through the gap of an old wooden hunting lodge door into a huge drawing room that had a large fireplace with a roaring fire in it; above the lintel of the fireplace hung a grand painting. There were three men standing around in suits, discussing a witch who they intended to burn. All the time, the chatter was getting louder and louder. She wanted to cover her ears but couldn't, and the pressure was getting heavier and heavier. She tried to cry to Paul for help but couldn't, and was frozen with fear.

Then it stopped! Luna shot bolt upright in bed, sweating and shaking all over. She'd never been so frightened in her life. She woke Paul to tell him of her ordeal, and the decision was made that they had to move. Not long after this they moved out of the house that had haunted them, but the vision still stays with Luna to this day.

Old Woolworths Store

In the early 1980s, a lady from Doncaster was working for Woolworths as a cleaner. One day, whilst cleaning the staff toilets, she was surprised to see a man wearing Victorian dress – consisting of a long-tailed coat and pinstriped trousers, complete with felt top hat – standing in the ladies' toilets. Taken aback by the gentleman's presence, she soon went about scolding him for being there – but instead of defending his actions, he just smiled and tipped his hat at the woman and evaporated into thin air. The cleaner was so scared that she reported the matter to her manager, but he just laughed at her and refused to believe her encounter. With this, the woman left her job and vowed never to return. Other staff working at the store also reported the man in the ladies' toilets, who smiled at them before disappearing into thin air.

Binns Department Store

The old Binns store in Doncaster closed down in 2008 and reopened as a House of Fraser. Many people will remember that the original store had a restaurant in the basement that served Doncaster's shoppers over the years. However, the breaking of pots and pans wasn't just from the staff there. Numerous reports were made of a poltergeist that used to throw things around, even when custom-

The former WoolWorths Shop where the ghost of a man has been seen dressedin a top hat an tails. (Authors' collection)

ers were in the shop. Things got so bad that the management brought in a Pentecostal parishioner, who performed an exorcism on the place to try to calm things down – but the malevolent activity continued until the restaurant was closed and the area became part of the new store. It would be interesting to know if the haunting continues today.

Odeon Cinema

The curtain finally fell on Doncaster's Odeon cinema in 2008, after seventy-four years of entertainment – but it left a legacy of ghost sightings. Reports have been made from staff and customers alike of a black figure running up and down the stairwell. One of the acts back in the 1950s reported that the black figure had approached them one evening whilst they were waiting to get ready backstage. When the black spectre turned to face the frightened artiste, they couldn't see its face, just a hole where its face should have been. The artiste screamed out in fear, but the mysterious apparition just disappeared.

Throughout its time as a cinema, one of the seats in Screen One, opposite the men's toilets, was reported to fold down each time a new film was played, as if someone was watching the premiere. One of the workers there claimed to have seen a 'black blob' sitting in the seat.

Unfortunately, the property has now been demolished, leaving a large open space and taking all of its stories with it.

Doncaster High School for Girls

It seems as though one former student was reluctant to leave the old grammar school. Many children reported seeing a young girl crying where the main school hall used to be situated. She was said to be wearing an old pinafore-type dress and holding her hands over her face, sobbing. Students and teachers asked if the girl was ok, but, before the girl responded, she just faded away leaving the unsuspecting witnesses bewildered and shocked. It is not known who the girl was as there doesn't seem to be any reported deaths in the school's history. For some unknown reason she was always spotted in the same place.

The building is now closed as a school and is waiting to be developed into a new luxury office building. Will the girl be seen in the new offices?

St James' Swimming Pool

During renovations, an apparition was seen in the building. He is described as wearing Edwardian dress, complete with grand moustache and pipe. The man appears to be a very distinguished gentleman and on occasions tilts his hat to unsuspecting pool-users.

Corn Exchange

In the middle of Doncaster Market stands the 1870s' Corn Exchange, now restored and refurbished after a serious fire in 1994. In 1995, an archaeological excavation revealed a number of burials associated with the graveyard of the medieval church of St Mary Magdalene. Numerous skeletons were unearthed, some dating back to the late fifteenth/early sixteenth century. Other finds included pottery, glass, clay pipe and animal bone.

Multiple ghosts were seen here in the early hours of the day, years before these finds were uncovered, but the most common phenomenon is the sound of chatter echoing through the vast hall, long into the night.

The former school, where a ghostly girl has been seen. (Authors' collection)

Ghost sightings were reported here and skeletal remains were dug up. (Authors' collection)

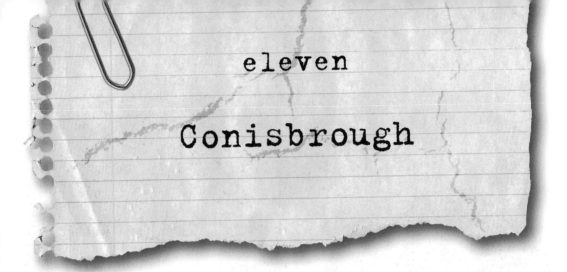

eleven

Conisbrough

A Village Built on a Burial Ground

During our research, it became apparent that Conisbrough town centre is highly charged in supernatural energy. This is hardly surprising given that St Peter's graveyard dates back over 1,250 years and originally stretched from Elm Green Lane to the priory, covering what is now the centre of Conisbrough.

The oldest building in South Yorkshire. (Authors' collection)

The priory during its use as an orphanage. In the early 1960s, bodies were unearthed here. (Photograph courtesy of Conisbrough & Denaby Main Heritage Group)

During the 1960s, the graveyard was reduced in size to widen the road between the church and the Fox public house, and it was during this time that a morbid discovery was made. A council worker uncovered plague victims that were stacked twelve deep; they had been entombed behind walls and stairwells in the priory. They also found a room in the basement that resembled an old chapel, complete with wine dating back to the sixteenth century. The room is reputedly haunted by a group of small children and the figure of a religious man.

Creepy Conisbrough Castle

Tunnels to Doncaster and Tickhill are said to run from the bottom of the keep.

Over the years, numerous local historical landmarks have claimed to be connected to the castle via such tunnels. These have included Tickhill Castle, Roche Abbey in Maltby, and numerous buildings in Hooton Roberts, along with the catacombs in Doncaster.

The Black Friar

Conisbrough Castle is a place of legends. Friars and phantoms are said to walk the battlements, scaring visitors and locals alike. The first reported sighting seems to date back to the 1770s, when a local, walking through the castle grounds one morning, saw the hooded figure gliding through the battlements. Shaken by what he saw, he contacted the local newspaper.

This extract comes from the *Lyonnell Copley Chronicles* of 1779:

On the night before today
In castle built of Conisbro stone
Myne eyes have seen phantom
Of Abbot Monk alowne
In the castel with a candel lyt
He was only in Castel chapel
Wore he dyd noy syt
Ome at Mecesboro
Betty my wife I towld of the phantom and
  she spowk.
No mower must you spake now of them
  fantommy fowk.
I was cauld, caulder then fust man that deed,
And scayed, but I be not scayed or cauld no
  mower.
O pray for the cursed Cunisbro Abbott
  Monk that wrought this hour to me!
May the lord take pitty on hym and take me
  wen I dee.

(Richard Glafsby)

Over the years there have been a number of similar sightings in the grounds, including a comparatively recent one in March 1994, when a local man saw what he described as a caped figure ascending the castle keep just outside the curtain wall. Although it was dark, the street lighting on the surrounding roads illuminated the side of the castle enough for him to see the shadowy figure against the stone background. He said that it climbed about halfway to the top before moving sideways out of sight and around to the other side. His girlfriend at the time also witnessed the event.

He has tried to rationalise the sighting for many years but still can't believe that a person can climb that particular section of the keep in the way that he witnessed and at such an alarming speed. He has lived in Conisbrough for nearly twenty years and

Conisbrough Castle with Wilsons Mill (now the Mill Piece) in the foreground. (Photograph courtesy of Conisbrough & Denaby Main Heritage Group)

has been to the castle at all times of day and night, but has never again seen anything like what he saw that night.

The White Lady

Many other sightings have occurred within the keep itself. The figure of a woman is said to fall from the keep battlements at the side facing Burcroft Hill. Witnesses describe her as wearing a flowing white gown. She circles the battlements before screaming as she falls to her death. Eyewitnesses have heard her ear-piercing scream before seeing a white figure falling and disappearing behind the trees. It is only after they have gone to investigate the horrific sight that they have realised there is no body to be found. It is not known who the woman was, or whether she was pushed or threw herself off. We have been unable to trace a recorded death of this nature.

Some suggest that this is the same woman who haunts the Lady Chapel off the master bedroom in the keep, where witnesses have felt a presence and heard the sounds of a woman's pitiful sobbing. Outside, numerous Conisbrough residents have seen lights through the window of the chapel at night. Most believe that a light has been left on in the castle, but true believers adamantly claim that it's the candlelight of the Lady in White, praying before her untimely demise.

It has been claimed that she is the ghost of Countess de Warrenne, who was murdered by her husband in the castle chapel. Her body is thought to have been boarded up in the Norman stronghold, but has never been found.

The curtain wall where the monk was seen. (Authors' collection)

The side of the castle where the White Lady is said to fall. (Authors' collection)

We were fortunate enough to be invited in for the evening to investigate the alleged sightings. During the investigation, one member of the team saw a pair of grey transparent legs ascending the staircase to the roof; no one else was there at the time. Also, during a lone vigil, a ball of light appeared on camera then shot across the room; a loud bang was then heard that shook the floor. Another member of the team experienced a bizarre and unnerving event: whilst filming, he was grabbed on the shoulder by an invisible hand, and then heard a groan followed by heavy breathing in his ear, freezing him to the spot with fear. Upon reviewing the video footage that was taken at the time, we could clearly hear the sound of a long groan followed by a heavy breathing sound. This was unheard by other members at the time.

During our investigation, we discovered that in the evening all of the power to the castle is switched off from a main switch in the visitors' centre. So why do so many people see a light coming from within the chapel? Richard Glafsby also refers to the light in the chapel, and the poem would have pre-dated any artificial lighting. This seems to dispel the theory that someone has left a light on by mistake …

We also learned that many years ago, during the 1940s, Revd Hutchinson of the Wesley Methodist Chapel, Conisbrough, conducted the first exorcism at the castle to get rid of a monastic spirit. He and others believed that he did a fine job of the exorcisms too; however, although reduced, the sightings still continue to this day.

Carr Lane Capers

Phantom Cavalier

Back in the 1960s, there was a caravan site near the entrance to Crookhill Hall. A young local man was dating a girl from the site and, after spending the evening with her babysitting, the girl's parents came home and it was time for him to leave. He set off on his hurried walk home, hunching his shoulders against the wind on the unusually dark night. Following the footpath to the woods, he could see the curtain wall of the old stone cottage known as the 'Hob Loft'. The footpath begins to narrow as it approaches the main building – which is situated on the corner of a bad bend, forcing walkers onto the road. The footpath has since been widened due to the hazard of pedestrians being hit on the blind bend.

As he reached the corner of the building where the path narrows, a man came around the bend from the opposite direction. The man was wearing a long riding cloak and a large hat bearing a white ostrich feather plume; he almost bumped into him. The young man stepped aside to allow the stranger to pass; he bid the man goodnight, but received no response.

Taking a second to register what he had seen, the young man rationalised that the stranger must be coming back from a fancy-dress party and he turned to have another look – only to discover that the man in his Cavalier costume had vanished off the face of the earth, with nowhere to go.

Even though this story is over fifty years old, we managed to track down the young man in question and interview him. We then went to investigate the area of the sighting and can confirm that there is no possible escape route for the Cavalier to have taken in the time frame described. Even though the man was ridiculed by friends and family alike, he still maintains this story to date.

Crookhill Hall in its heyday.

High Spirits on Carr Lane

In the mid-1960s, a group of local farm-hands, who had been drinking in the Plough Inn at Micklebring, claimed to have had a paranormal accident on Carr Lane on their way home.

The four friends left the Plough Inn at around 12 o'clock one Friday evening and set off home. Their spirits were high as they laughed and joked about the evening's events. As they came round the sharp bend on Carr Lane towards the entrance to Crookhill Hall, a young girl in long, white, flowing robes emerged out of the entrance of the old Crookhill Hall grounds, straight into their path. Everyone saw the girl and shouted to the driver to look out. The driver swerved the car to the right to miss the girl but lost control, causing the vehicle to snake in a zigzag motion. The car then rebounded off the wall and ploughed through the adjacent hedge, landing in the field nearby.

Fortunately, no one was hurt. Shaken, they climbed out of the car and quickly tried to search for the girl to see if she was ok. But after calling out for a while and searching nearby, no trace of her could be found. They left the car in the hedge and returned the following morning, still shocked at what they had witnessed the previous night. At the time, several people claiming to have been passengers in the vehicle came forward, but no one has ever admitted to being the driver.

Site of an accident black spot. (Authors' collection)

Over the years, numerous cars have gone through the same hedge, claiming to have had the same experience.

Crookhill Hall

This seventeenth-century hall was considerably altered in the late eighteenth century, and became a tuberculosis sanatorium after the Second World War. Many returning servicemen, suffering from shellshock or physical disabilities, were also housed in TB hospitals – often dying on-site, after contracting TB themselves. When the sanatorium finally closed, the empty building was damaged by vandalism and fire, resulting in its demolition in 1968. Later, the grounds became a golf course. Surprisingly, it is not the ghost of an ex-soldier or tuberculosis victim that has been spotted in the area.

A distraught wailing woman has been seen running from the site of the former hall down what is known as the 'Fairway', between the first and tenth hole. On the Fairway, a bell is situated on a tree for golfers to ring to warn other players when they're taking a shot. Witnesses say that the crying woman rings the bell as she passes and heads off towards the old cottage known as the 'Hob Loft' before disappearing. Golfers often hear the bell ring when the evening is drawing in, even though they know that there is no one playing that hole.

The bell that is heard ringing. (Authors' collection)

Cromwells Restaurant

A short distance from St Peter's Church in Conisbrough there stands an unusual old building which appears at first glance to be Georgian in origin. A closer inspection of the property's architecture reveals that the old house, now a restaurant called Cromwells, has much earlier roots, and is believed to have been built during the 1600s. The building has had many uses – such as a farmhouse, a boarding school, a post office, and a community centre. In 1983, it was sold on to become the restau-rant that we see today. Soon after the sale, a rather unexpected visitor from the past was handed down along with the deeds of the property, much to the surprise of the cur-rent owners and staff.

The restaurant's chef reported that one of the waiters was startled by a figure in a long cloak and a large hat with a feather sticking out of it, who rushed past him as he made his way down the stairs. The figure, described as being similar in appearance to a Cavalier, disappeared in an instant. Also, on occasion, kitchen doors have been slammed on unsuspecting staff,

Cromwells as it stands today. (Authors' collection)

causing them to drop handfuls of plates and cutlery.

In 1989, when renovations were taking place, an electrician was rewiring in the upper part of the building in semi-darkness. He was so convinced that a man had walked past him and disappeared that he dropped his tools and ran downstairs to confront his colleague, whom he suspected of playing tricks. His workmate assured him that this was not the case; it was only then that the electrician realised that the figure he had seen had been wearing what he guessed to be sixteenth-century dress, with sacking gaiters on his legs. The building was used periodically as a working farmhouse for more than 200 years. The dress of the apparition suggests that he was a land worker, and his appearance has since been recorded on several occasions by unsuspecting visitors to the restaurant.

A worker was preparing to close the premises at the end of a busy evening, when all except two of the guests had left the downstairs restaurant. Without warning, a huge gust of air screeched past their heads and 'banged' into the wall close to the chimney. Although the sound was so loud that the remaining guests left in terror, nothing was physically seen, and no explanation could be found.

Another local legend tells how one of the former occupants of the building was involved in an affair with a local man. When her husband found out, she is said to have hanged herself from one of the ceiling beams near the stairs. Could the screeching be caused by the lost soul of the woman who hanged herself in shame over her illicit affair?

The Star

Margaret

The Star Hotel in Conisbrough was originally a coaching inn on the main road from Sheffield to Doncaster, before it burned down in 1909. It was soon rebuilt in 1910 – as good as new, only this time it came with a ghost.

On Sunday, 31 October 1909, the Star Hotel caught fire, engulfing the timber-framed building. The landlord evacuated everyone into the street and awaited help. It was only then that he realised fourteen-year-old Margaret Evelyn Mountford, a maid working there, was still inside. Horrified onlookers could see Margaret at the bedroom window, screaming for help. In a brave attempt to rescue the girl, the landlord raced back into the building and tried to reach her, but was cut off by the staircase, which was now fully ablaze. He shouted to Margaret to get back into the front bedroom and promised that he would get a ladder to rescue her.

After several minutes, a ladder was sourced and a second attempt to free her was made. Smashing the windowpane, they shouted, 'Margaret!', but no reply was heard and by this time the room was thick with smoke. Several attempts were made to enter the building via the window, but the brave men were beaten back by the flames. In the end all they could do was stand back and watch as the once grand structure became her funeral pyre. By the following morning, all that was left was a pile of rubble and cinders.

Many people have seen what they describe as a pretty young girl with long dark hair, looking out of the upstairs window with the curtains pulled aside, crying. Members of staff have often seen the same girl dressed in turn-of-the-cen-

The Star Hotel before the fire. Could the lady in the window be Margaret? (Photograph courtesy of Conisbrough & Denaby Main Heritage Group)

tury attire, crying at the top of the stairs. Could this be Margaret, still trapped after that fateful day back in 1909?

A Regular Haunt at Christmas Time

On Christmas Eve 1914, not long after burying a close friend, two regulars went to the Star, just as they used to do every year with their late friend. They ordered a round as they normally did and took their usual seats; it was a sorry sight indeed to see the empty third chair at their table.

All of a sudden they heard a familiar voice and looked towards the main door, which opened and then closed without anyone entering or leaving. They looked at each other, then again at the door, and, in a bid to raise their spirits, joked that it must be their deceased friend who had come to drink with them one more time.

Suddenly, almost as if in response to their joke, the lights went out and they heard a distinct baritone voice sing the opening verse of their friend's favourite song: 'It's a long way to Tipperary'; as the voice faded, the lights returned. The two friends cheered at the possibility that their friend was with them, and each bought him a pint, placing them at his empty seat.

They spent the night fondly talking as if their friend was still sat with them, even to the point of ribbing him about not having drunk his first pint by calling time. As they were about to leave, they said, 'I suppose we better drink these for you then.' As they lifted the two glasses from

Highfield Road today. (Authors' collection)

his place, they were shocked but pleasantly surprised to find a note underneath each drink. The first read, 'God bless you all, Merry Christmas', and the other read, 'Sorry I couldn't stay lads, it's the thought that counts.'

High Antics of Highfields Road

All names and property details have been changed or withheld to protect the identity of those involved, including the current owners.

As a child of six years old, Martin lived for a short time in a small house with his grandparents, sister, mother and stepfather. The house was overcrowded, but it wasn't long before a house on the same road came up for sale. The house had been empty for around a year before they went to look at it, but even then stories of it being haunted were rife amongst locals and it was quite well-known.

Shortly before his parents went to view the property, Martin had a nightmare about the place. He dreamt that he and his sister were playing hide-and-seek in the house; she went into the bathroom and said that there was no one there, and then went into a bedroom to the right. Martin decided to double check and peered around the door. He then stood inside the bathroom with the door shut and saw a woman sat in the bath with her wrist cut. The bath was full of blood; blood was also streaming down her face and she was staring right into Martin's eyes. Martin was paralysed with fear and it seemed an eternity before he woke up, shaking with fright at the nightmare.

Shortly after this, Martin's parents took possession of the house and Martin saw the place for the first time. To his surprise, the house was the same layout as it had been in his dream, even though he had never been there before.

The house was originally built as two houses, but over the years the property had been knocked into one and was referred to as the Highfields House; it was divided again into two before the rest of the street was erected. The property had a Gothic Victorian feel, with twin bay windows at either side of a shared passageway. Upon entering the front door, there was an old parquet floor that used to click underfoot. It was a darkened hallway with a stained wood finish and decorated in a Tudor style. Opposite the door was a dim stairwell covered in a deep-red plush carpet; leading off to the right-hand side was a glass door into the front living room. At the back of the property was an open-plan lounge-cum-kitchen area. On the second floor, at the top of the stairs, was an old wooden door which led into the bathroom. To the immediate right was the doorway leading into the back bedroom, with a window facing the back of the properties behind. Down a corridor was the front master bedroom, small box room and a storage cupboard. The top of the stairs was only ever lit with a single bulb covered by a red lampshade, which didn't provide much light during the hours of darkness.

The house had a strange, sinister feel, like somebody was always there, watching. The family moved in and began to settle in to their new life. Martin was issued the small box room next to his parents' room and his sister occupied the rear bedroom that overlooked the backyard.

Memories of the nightmare about the bathroom stuck in Martin's mind and he often shuddered as he passed it. He would reach the point of bursting before he would venture to the bathroom after dark, along the dimly lit landing that was bathed in the crimson light. He would never look into the bath, in fear of his nightmare coming true.

A number of weeks after moving in, Martin heard footsteps coming along the landing towards his bedroom door and then stopping. He shouted for his mother, but she told him that no one had been there and it was his imagination. This went on for several weeks and his mother quickly lost patience with Martin's constant cries for help. She scolded him for having disturbed her sleep. The intensity increased to such a point that he began sneaking into his parents' room, too afraid to be alone. This caused more upset in the household; his stepfather tried to blame his overactive imagination on the Catholic school he attended and decided that Martin should move schools. He also put a lock on their bedroom door to keep Martin out. Now Martin was left alone in his room to suffer the nightly occurrences of footsteps heading towards him and creaking floorboards.

Things took a turn for the worse one night when his stepfather was working nights and his mother was staying in his sister's room due to her being ill. Again the footsteps started, but, unlike before, they didn't stop; they continued to pace up and down outside the door. This was followed by the squeaking sound of the door handle being turned. Frozen with fear, Martin sat there with his arms around his knees, moving back and forwards in a rocking motion, transfixed by the door and praying. Silence fell upon the house when the noises slowly petered out. However, Martin was still too scared to move and waited at least another hour before he dared head towards the door and seek safety with his mother and sister at the opposite end of the house. Plucking up his courage, he turned the door handle; he could hear the mechanisms move in the lock, the same noise he had heard before. Finally, the click of the lock released the door from the frame and he began to pull the door inwards, peering wide-eyed into the dark, red hallway.

Taking a deep breath, he repeated the words his stepfather had often told him: 'There's no such thing as ghosts.' Pushing himself, he stepped into the hallway, feeling the soft carpet under his bare feet. Grabbing hold of the banister rail, he edged his way towards his sister's room through the darkness, knowing he had to pass the bathroom to reach sanctuary. He turned his back to the bathroom door and pushed open the bedroom door. Entering the room, he stood at the corner of the four-poster bed, which was draped in netting and tied back with ribbons; he could see that his sister was asleep in front of him and that his mother was to the right of her. Knowing he would be scolded if he woke any of them, he proceeded towards the side where his mother was sleeping, hoping to sneak into the bed.

As he moved around the bottom of the bed, a blue glint of light caught his eye and distracted him. He stood still whilst trying to focus on it – it was the shape of a small torso. Again he said to himself, 'There's no such thing as ghosts', and reasoned that it was probably a nightgown hung on the wardrobe door. Continuing

towards the safety of his mother, he got to the foot of the bed before noticing that the shape had now grown to the size of an evening gown. Transfixed, he watched as it began to develop like an old-fashioned Polaroid photograph, growing in size and detail, finally forming into a woman floating about a foot off the floor with her head bowed down. Martin describes her as being in her late twenties with long ringlets of hair, which appeared to be wet, covering her face. She was dressed in a nightgown with puffed-out sleeves that were hanging loosely off her forearms, exposing her wrists and hands; he could even see the fine lace detailing around the neck area of the gown. Just below her bust, the material draped loosely towards the ground.

Martin's mind was blank at this point and he felt his body moving towards the figure as if being drawn towards her by some invisible force. When he got within a few feet from her, she lifted her head and reached out her arms towards him. Dumbstruck, he stepped backwards and let out a primeval roar – not made by a conscious decision but just a pure scream of absolute terror!

With this, his mother bolted upright in bed and inadvertently jumped between Martin and the Lady in White, who she had not seen. Bending down to eye level, she started to shout at Martin, 'Don't you ever come into this room and do that again!', wagging her finger with every syllable. But Martin was still staring at the woman behind her, still screaming – until the point where his mother struck his left arm to make him stop. It was only then that Martin even realised his mother was there. He could still see the figure that had terrified him so much, and this was more frightening than any of his mother's

threats. The impact of the blow had only distracted him for a split second as he could still see the woman – who was now beginning to dissolve into a whirlwind-shaped mist. She had disappeared before his mother had a chance to turn around and see what he was staring at.

Stuttering, Martin tried to explain what he had seen, but his mother stated that he must have been having a nightmare. Martin knew that what he had seen was no dream. Scolding him for causing panic, she sent Martin to bed – but he couldn't face another moment in that room and, in the morning, his stepfather returned home from work and found him sat on the sofa.

Even though his parents didn't believe what Martin saw, they did try to help him settle more at night by staying in his room and reading to him. They also provided him with a television, something that kids didn't have in their rooms back then. They even took him to the doctors to get something to help calm him down. Martin still insisted that they were not alone in the house, and, after the sighting, the phenomena got worse. The footsteps now occurred on a nightly basis, but were now also accompanied by the sound of fingernails being dragged down the paint-work and a long, drawn-out, hushed voice calling his name, 'M-A-R-T-I-N … M-A-R-T-I-N …' repeatedly. He was unable to sleep until eventually he would pass out with exhaustion. Finally, he and his parents could take no more and they agreed that he should move back in with his grand-parents, who lived a few doors away.

At twelve years old, Catherine knew that the house was haunted, but no one ever talked of it; the subject was taboo, especially after her brother moved to her grandparents' house. Even her friend, Sherry, who lived across the road, would tease and say that she could see an old woman rocking in an old chair in her bedroom window.

Catherine frequently felt a presence and knew she wasn't alone; however, she wasn't disturbed by it at first. When she returned home from university, at the age of twenty, her room had been empty for two years. She decided to redecorate in a Gothic style and found an old pack of tarot cards. She put some of the cards on her wall, but didn't realise that this would cause things to take a turn for the worse.

She started to notice that the noises she had heard as a child and dismissed were now louder and more intense; the footsteps became more frequent on the parquet floor downstairs and every little noise began to get louder and louder, as if the spirit was getting stronger.

One night, Catherine was alone in her bedroom when her thoughts were broken by the sound of what she describes as a cat scratching on a wicker basket; this seemed strange as Catherine had neither a cat nor a wicker basket. She got out of bed and turned on the light to see what the noise could be, but the noise had stopped. Scared at this, she decided to leave the light on, as she could feel the atmosphere beginning to get heavier and darker. She sensed that she was not alone, and began to feel the sensation of impending doom.

Catherine looked around the room to see what had made the noise. As she scanned the room, she cast her gaze over a picture board that she had on the wall. All of a sudden it seemed to move. Thinking it was her eyes playing tricks on her, she glanced away for a second, when the frame suddenly flew off the wall and smashed on the floor, scattering the photos amongst the splintered wood. The picture board had been hung on the wall for a number of years and there was no reason for it to fall suddenly like it did.

Thinking this was a sign that something bad was going to happen, Catherine woke up her mother to tell her what had taken place. Her mother came to her room to help tidy up the broken frame and photos, and noticed that amongst the photos, face down, lay a tarot card. She picked it up and turned it over; it was 'The Fool' card. Laughing at this, her mother said that she had been made a fool of, and said, 'There is no wonder your imagination's running away with you when you've got rubbish like this in your room.'

The atmosphere in the house began to get even more oppressive after this and the noises and footsteps that had once plagued Martin had clearly found a new victim. Catherine kept insisting to her mother that they were not alone and that the house was indeed haunted like her brother had stated years before. Eventually, her mother yielded to her pleas and decided to spend the night in her bedroom to prove that there was nothing to worry about.

At around 3 a.m., the footsteps once again began to stalk the corridors. Catherine was instantly frozen with fear as the footsteps reached the door; in a hushed voice, she called out to her mother and tried to nudge her awake without alarming the entity. But no matter how hard she tried, she couldn't wake her mother. The entity seemed to realise what was happening and took great delight in increasing the terror factor by swinging the door back and forth whilst creaking the floorboards, until eventually slamming the door shut with an almighty bang, shaking the room. This finally stirred Catherine's mother, who rolled over. Catherine said, 'You must have heard that.'

Her mother replied, 'It's just the heating banging, go back to sleep.'

Catherine couldn't take much more and decided to leave the house the following day, vowing never to return. However, she still had some property left inside the house. She was so scared that she asked Martin to go with her to collect it. They went to the house when everyone was out at work but Catherine was concerned at what might happen whilst there, so told Martin to leave the door unlocked in case they needed to make a quick escape. They headed upstairs to Catherine's room and Catherine told Martin to keep watch on the landing, fearing that they might both get locked in. She began to pack frantically in case the entity came whilst they were there. Whilst she was packing, Martin made the comment, 'What do you think it's going to do? Lock us in?'

'Don't make fun of it whilst we're in the house,' Catherine said.

Martin replied, 'Now you know how I felt all those years ago.'

After packing, they retreated back down the stairs and headed towards the front door, but the key wasn't in the lock where Catherine had left it. Martin asked Catherine where the key had gone but she told him to stop messing about. Martin slowly turned around, ashen-faced, and slowly said, 'Catherine … it's locked!'

Catherine screamed and panicked, throwing her belongings onto the floor. Martin remembered that there was a key in the back door and hurried her through the house to escape. Once outside, she begged Martin to go back in and collect her belongings whilst she held the back door open for him.

After this, Catherine consulted with a local psychic, who convinced her that she could clear the spirit from the house if she performed a smudging. 'Smudging' is the common name given to a powerful cleansing technique through the burning of sage. It is a ceremonial way to cleanse a person, place or an object of negative energies or influences.

However, all did not go as planned. The psychic mocked the entity, which only angered it to the point where it tipped an old wardrobe over, sending it crashing to the floor. The noise echoed around the house and the psychic turned on her heels and fled the house, with Catherine in hot pursuit.

Several months later, Catherine's mother was hosting a coffee evening with some friends; she was next door visiting neighbours when a taxi pulled up with her guests. Going out to greet them, her friend said, 'For an awful moment, I thought you lived there,' pointing at her house. Curious, but not giving away that she lived there, she asked what was wrong with the house.

Her friend replied, 'I used to live there with my mother, it's haunted.' She proceeded to tell her that things had got so bad one night that the entity had climbed in bed with her mother, frightening her to death and forcing them to flee in the middle of the night. Within a month, they had handed the keys back and moved out, terrified at what they had witnessed.

It finally dawned on Catherine's mother that her children had been telling the truth all along. She knew she had to take a stand and called in the local vicar from St Peter's Church, who performed a blessing on the house in a bid to rid it of the evil. The property was sold soon after this, and to date there have been no reports of paranormal activity from the new owners.

A view over the valley where the White Lady is seen. (Authors' collection)

Lady's Valley

Northcliffe Quarry is known locally as Lady's Valley, as a White Lady has been seen there on numerous occasions throughout the years. Some of the sightings date back to the turn of the century. The cause of her death has been lost in the passage of time, and all that remains is her ghost – a whispered memory of her tragic death.

Legend says that if you go to the quarry on the night of a full moon at witching hour, she will appear in a moonlit dance and, if you catch her eyes, you'll be condemned to remain with her forever. Over the years the site has also been used for gypsy bare-knuckle fighting, pagan meetings and prostitution due to its discrete location. Quite a grim past for such a picturesque place!

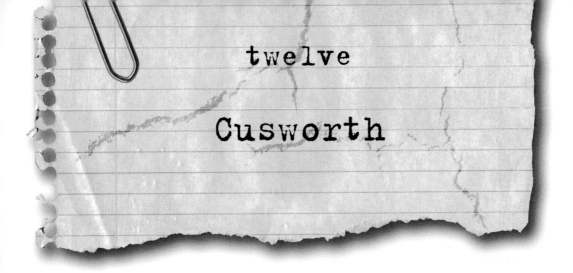

twelve

Cusworth

Cusworth Hall Haunting

The eighteenth-century Cusworth Hall was once home to the Battie-Wrightson family. The hall has since been converted into a museum and is said to be haunted by a number of individual spirits. These include the ghost of a lady who is seen sitting with a cane, in a black dress and ivory shawl, peering out of an upstairs window. Visitors and guests have asked staff who the woman is, only to discover that there is no one in the building fitting that description.

A visiting family had another strange encounter at the hall when they heard the haunting music of a phantom piano. The family said that it was quite unnerving and sounded so real. They followed the music down the corridor and up the stairs until they could clearly hear it coming from behind a bedroom door. They slowly opened the door, expecting to see a piano recital, only to find an empty room; the music had abruptly stopped. Returning to their tour, they asked a member of staff about the room and recounted their experience, only to be told that it was the same room where the lady has been seen peering out of the window.

Other unsuspecting visitors have seen a man standing by the grand fireplace, as if greeting guests into his home. He soon fades away, leaving them doubting their own sanity.

In the base of the house there is an old classroom. Children have been seen and heard in this area, running and screaming with laughter through the corridors and into the rooms, but upon investigation the rooms are empty.

We did speak to a security guard at the hall, who told us that the stories of the hauntings were made up by a previous owner to encourage visitors. But those who know the place have to admit that there's something not quite right about old Cusworth Hall.

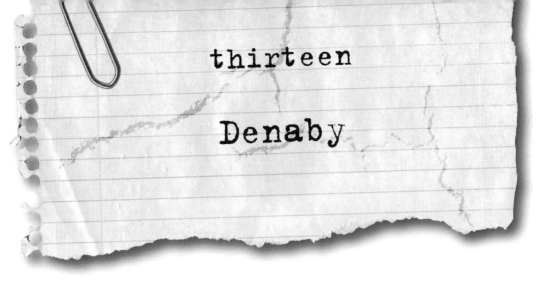

thirteen

Denaby

Faceless Figure of Denaby Crags

The Crags are a chain of north-facing slopes forming one side of a 'funnel' leading into the Don Gorge. Numerous sightings have occurred on the cinder paths between Conisbrough and St Alban's Church, Denaby. Here are two such accounts:

The footpath from St Alban's Church that heads towards Conisbrough. (Authors' collection)

One autumn evening, some time in the 1920s, a local boy was riding his bike home down the Crags when he saw a man dressed in a tweed suit and flat cap walking up the winding path towards him. He appeared to be looking at the floor as he laboured his way up the hill. Worried that he was going to be late home, the boy called out to the approaching man, "As tha got time on thi clock?' The man looked up in response and, to the boy's horror, revealed that he had no face. Screaming with terror, the boy sped off down the Crags at full pelt, looking over his shoulder at the faceless man. It was only when he got to St Alban's Church that the ghost vanished from sight. But the boy didn't stop or slow down until he reached home, where he ran into the kitchen to tell his mam and dad what had happened.

In 1994, two girls were walking home up the Crags after babysitting one warm summer's evening when they noticed a man walking along the path behind them. They cautiously slowed down to let him pass, as they didn't like having a stranger behind them. As he got within a few yards of the girls, they stepped off the path to let him walk by – but, as he passed, they noticed that he had no facial features. Terrified, they scrambled up the Crags and ran home to tell their parents, who made a report to the police.

It is believed that there are many unreported sightings of this strange spectral figure, spanning decades of time. Many speculate that he is a former miner who is trying to get home after the 1912 Cadeby Pit disaster.

The Lantern Boy

The area has a history of coal mining dating back several hundred years, so it comes as no surprise that one of Denaby's best-known mining spectres has been wandering the landscape for over a century.

Children were once used as 'trappers', opening and closing wooden trapdoors underground to help air circulation in the tunnels. At the beginning of each shift they would be issued with a small piece of candle, and, when this burned out, they continued working in total darkness.

The Lantern Boy is believed to be the spirit of a trapper who died in a tragic accident in the 1800s. Until the middle of the twentieth century, sightings of the Lantern Boy were quite commonplace in and around isolated areas of Conisbrough and Denaby. The ghost was last seen around 1945 by a young man who was walking near the Crags, on the same footpath that is traversed by the faceless figure. The man described the spirit as wearing tattered clothes and carrying a bright light. At first he thought it was one of the local children heading home, until he realised that his attire was out of place and he didn't seem to be walking in a normal fashion – he described the boy as gliding through the long grass. Scared at this, the young man ran home.

Mexborough Ragger

Prior to her untimely death, a young gypsy girl was affectionately nicknamed the Mexborough Ragger, as she frequently walked through the streets of Mexborough calling out, 'Rag, rags, bring out your old rags.' It was common for gypsies to be termed raggers because they would collect rags from the richer households, then sort through them to sell on for a profit. Any clothing that was unfit for purpose would be sold to make mattresses and padding; all buttons and fastenings were removed to be sold on for a price.

The third arch – where you call out for the Mexborough Ragger. (Authors' collection)

It is said that she used to walk through a tunnel towards the quarry to sell the old shirts and work clothes to the quarry workers. On one such day, she walked her normal route through the tunnel – but she was hit by a train before she could get to the archway where she usually stood when the trains went past. She had heard the train coming but had slipped and dropped her goods. After scrambling to retrieve them she was too late to reach the sanctuary of the archway, and the freight train cut her to ribbons.

If you call out, 'Mexborough Ragger, Mexborough Ragger, Mexborough Ragger', she reappears, walking through the tunnel towards you as if she thinks you are calling to buy her wares. But caution should be taken before doing this as you might incur a gypsy curse. We went to this location and drew straws to see who would call out her name – we were relieved that the Mexborough Ragger did not appear to us!

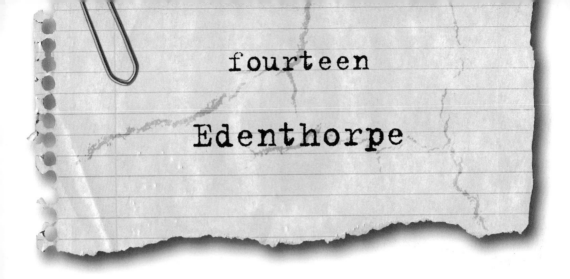

fourteen

Edenthorpe

Edenthorpe Entity

In 1922 a fire gutted the central block of Edenthorpe Hall, which was demolished as a result. The north wing was converted into a house and flats, and the south wing into a house. This wing was later used as a club library and from 1959 as an infants' school; however, it too was later demolished.

The burned-down central section of the hall is said to be haunted by the ghost of a daughter of the manor, who lost her life in the fire all those years ago. In the 1930s, children often reported seeing her wandering around where the floors in the central structure once stood. She was commonly known as the White Lady of Edenthorpe Hall. The White Lady is still said to haunt the site where the building once stood.

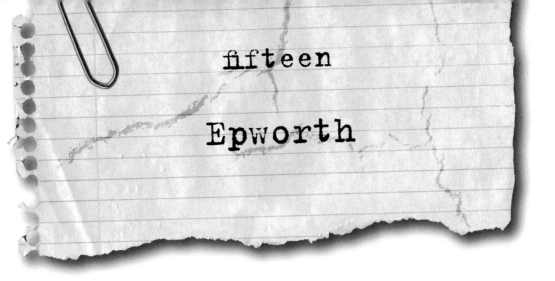

fifteen

Epworth

Epworth Rectory

Epworth's Old Rectory is famous as the haunt of one of Britain's best-known and best-documented poltergeists – Old Jeffrey. This ghost tormented the Wesleys, a family later made famous by John Wesley the preacher. John collected accounts of the ghost from various family members, but these weren't published until 1791. John was thirteen when he was subjected to the terrors of the ghost, which was named Old Jeffrey by his nineteen-year-old sister Hetty – who was even then suspected of being the medium or the cause of the phenomena. The disturbances centred around Hetty's bed and were marked by her convulsions, which occurred at the time of the hauntings. This story is taken from the family's surviving letters; the letters of John's sister Hetty are still missing to this day.

On 1 December, a maid working for the Wesleys first experienced the haunting; she heard several dismal groans at the door of the dining room, which she later described as akin to the groans of one expiring. This frightened the maid so much that she daren't leave her room after dark. It was initially thought that the ghost was Mr Turpine, a deceased friend. Mrs Wesley gave little heed to the maid's revelation and endeavoured to laugh her out of her fears.

A couple of days later, several members of the family heard a strange knocking and rapping around the house. This continued every evening for a fortnight; sometimes it was in the attic, but most commonly in the nursery where Hetty slept. At first, not much notice was taken of the noises and the family thought it was quite amusing that something supernatural was happening in their own house. In a letter, dated 16 February 1750, Emily Wesley wrote:

> Another thing is that wonderful thing called by us Jeffrey. You won't laugh at me for being superstitious if I tell you how certainly that something calls on me against any extraordinary new affliction; but so little is known of the invisible world that I am at least not able to judge whether it be friendly or an evil spirit.

The home of Old Jeffrey. (Authors' collection)

On one occasion, one of the family members went downstairs just after the clock had struck ten to lock the doors as normal. Just as they were going back upstairs, they heard a noise which they described as like someone throwing a scuttle full of coal onto the kitchen floor with a loud clatter. Frightened, they fetched another family member. They first checked the kitchen to see if there had been a bucket of coal spilled, but the kitchen floor was as clean as a whistle; they went on to check all the lower rooms, but nothing was out of order.

Over the next few days the noises seemed to increase in frequency and the family started to become more frightened of the house. They took to travelling around in pairs, fearing the unknown. At this point they were convinced that it was beyond the power of any living creature to make such strange and various noises, and believed that they were now dealing with the supernatural.

The supposed entity would systematically target family members who were alone by knocking loudly nine times just beside their bed; as the activity increased, the knocking was followed by a quick winding up of the jack in the fireplace of the room. With every occurrence, the poltergeist seemed to get stronger. The family would get up to investigate, but no perpetrator or explanation could ever be found.

The noises became so outrageous that one evening Samuel Wesley and his wife Susanna decided to check the stairs to see what was happening. Lighting a candle and holding on to each other, the two of them walked down the stairs. Just as they got to the bottom, one of them described the sensation of somebody emptying a bag of money at their feet, then they heard crashing amongst the bottles under the stairs as if they had been shattered into a thousand pieces. After checking, they discovered that all the bottles were still intact, leaving them even more confused about what they had heard. At family prayers, the phenomena became more sporadic. Samuel often tried to speak to the unknown entity when this happened but the only answer he received was two or three feeble moans.

The family sent for the local vicar, Mr Hoole, to witness what they'd been experiencing over the last few weeks. They sat up with the vicar and waited for the noises to begin. At two o'clock it all started with the sound of the jack in the fireplace, followed by two separate incidents of three knocks.

Mr Hoole then went to the nursery alone. The entity seemed to take delight in this challenge and escalated the haunting to unprecedented levels of violent outbursts. First the knocks began over and under the room where he lay, and then at the head of the children's beds. The rapping was very hard and loud, so that the bed shook under Mr Hoole. Then he felt something walk by the bedside, as if someone had brushed against the mattress in a long nightgown. The bangs were so loud that even the vicar's faith could not persuade him to stay in the room. He came out of the chamber confused and disturbed at what he had just witnessed.

Heading into the kitchen, the sound began again from the rooms above. Wanting to rationalise what was happening, he ascended the narrow stairs again but was stopped in his tracks by the sound of someone dragging their feet. By this point the rest of the family had joined him, and then a trailing noise was heard, like the rustling of a silk nightgown. This stopped and the knocking of the nursery's bed head started again. The vicar made his excuses and then left, still puzzled.

Further incidents followed after this; the sound of a deep groan could be heard and the banging noises became more violent. On one occasion, the Wesleys' daughter Nancy, who was fourteen at the time, was lifted up with the bed in which she sat. She leapt down and said that surely Old Jeffrey would not run away with her. She was persuaded to sit down again when the bed was lifted several times successively to a considerable height. The noise even affected the mastiff of the household; it whimpered in terror.

The noises continued for several weeks and then became less frequent, until they faded away leaving the family wondering what had been happening all those weeks in their house.

There is a conspiracy theory that the haunting did not end as quickly as the story suggests, but was in fact suppressed by John Wesley. The reason for him suppressing this chapter of his life was perhaps because of his newfound position as head of a new religious movement. It is thought that, after he started to become famous, John Wesley personally destroyed or hid all of his sister Hetty's letters where any reference was made to her consulting spirits or practising mediumship; he also reportedly forbid the family to speak on this matter again. It is rumoured that the hauntings continued for the remainder of their time in the house and it has even been suggested that it was the Devil trying to test the strength of a future religious leader.

St George's Church

After the new parish incumbent Revd Morgan had been welcomed by the parishioners of St George's Church, he retired to his quarters and settled down with the good book – when all of a sudden he was startled by a horrifying gurgling noise. He searched the building, fearing intruders, but could find no account for the noise. He retired to his room but couldn't sleep and felt very unsettled. At 3 a.m. the phenomenon re-occurred but was now much louder and more distressing than ever.

When his housekeeper arrived the following morning, she found the reverend ashen-faced and visibly shaken. She enquired about his health, upon which he recounted the bizarre happenings of the previous evening. She told him of a man who had often stayed over at the house with the intention of courting a previous vicar's youngest daughter. After plucking up the courage to ask for her hand in marriage, the daughter rejected his offer due to his low social standing. The man then politely excused himself and retired to his room, where he hanged himself from the rafters and was found swinging from the beams the following morning.

Revd Morgan also kept noticing a skull on top of a headstone, and on numerous occasions he returned it to the ground only to find it on top of the headstone the following day. One evening he was woken by shouts and banging on the vicarage door, and an agitated young soldier, who stood there in full uniform, told him that he had seen a ghostly spectre rise from a grave. He went on to say that the ghost had swiftly retreated through the gravestones and disappeared over a wall that dropped almost 20ft into the school playground. Insisting that the soldier took him to the grave, Revd Morgan was horrified to discover that it was the very same grave over which the skull stood sentry.

The vicarage has since been demolished and no further reports have been made.

Epworth Tap and Wine Bar

Nestled in the heart of the historic market town is The Epworth Tap. The building was once a sweetshop, until finally becoming the renowned restaurant and bistro it is today. The owners Steve and Sarah have run The Epworth Tap, as it is now known, since 2004.

Steve was working one busy Saturday night when he noticed a couple walking towards the bar. He acknowledged them and asked if they had been attended to; the man replied that they had. Steve noticed that they were smartly dressed, with the woman wearing a long black evening dress and well made up, and the gentleman wearing dark slacks, a cream-coloured bomber jacket and sporting a well-groomed beard. Satisfied that they were being served, he proceeded through into a back room. Upon his return, he asked where the couple had gone. The bar tender, who had been there the whole time, was a little confused as to who Steve was referring to. After Steve had described the couple, the bar tender said that no one of that description had been in that evening. Steve, to this day, cannot understand what he saw.

Steve is not the only one who has witnessed strange things here. His wife Sarah, whilst standing at the bar, has on numerous occasions seen a dark figure ascending the staircase through a mirror that's facing the stairs. When she looks over to the stairs, there is no one there. In addition to this, one night after closing, Sarah was cleaning up before she went home when she noticed garden peas on the stairs. This might not sound unusual at a restaurant, but what confused Sarah was that the restaurant doesn't – and hasn't ever – sold peas.

There are numerous other stories about the ghost that lives in the building. Over the years, owners and visitors have reported the feeling of being watched late at night. A medium recently visited the bar and said that the ghost of an old regular sits at the bar, describing him as a 'grumpy old git'.

sixteen

Gringley on the Hill

The Cannon Ball Run

Just off the B1403 in Doncaster there is a lane known locally as the Cannon Ball Run. A couple in a parked car once watched a soldier wearing a hat march by their vehicle before vanishing in the beam of their headlights.

On a warm autumn day in 1976, a man was travelling down the B1403 when all of a sudden his bike broke down. He walked to a telephone box to contact his father so he could recover him and the bike. It was around 6 p.m. before his father arrived and the night was light and warm. His father loaded the bike into the van and they set off home.

Just before they got to the last corner, heading up to Beacon Hill, they were surprised to see in the headlights what they described as a white figure standing in the middle of the road. As they got closer, they could see it was a young lady, beckoning them to come towards her with her left hand. The father slowed down as he approached the woman and they could

both clearly see that she was smiling. What was more surprising was that her flowing white gown was 8–10in from the floor and no feet were visible.

The father, shocked and in disbelief, accelerated past the entity. She retreated backwards with an angry scowling face and headed off through a closed iron farm gate. Her pace quickened across the field until she was almost a blur and she vanished into the hillside. Lengthy discussions followed between the man and his father about what they had just witnessed, with the father refusing to believe what he had seen.

The family have since travelled the road on numerous occasions and have seen the ghost a further two times, but several years apart. However, the sightings have always been around autumn.

Since then a bus has crashed in the same spot. The driver was travelling down the hill when he swerved to miss 'a woman in white' who was standing in the road. Following the crash, he and his passengers got off to see if the woman was ok, but she couldn't be found.

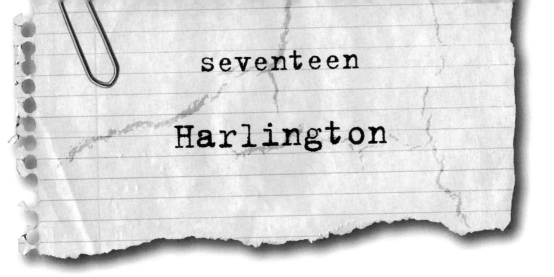

seventeen

Harlington

Harlington Hobo

Approximately thirty years ago, on a dark, cold night, a group of friends were having their usual wander around the village of Harlington. As they walked along the road from the village to the Crown Inn, they noticed in the distance the silhouette of a man approaching. As he got closer, they noticed that the man was dressed in 1940s' work attire, consisting of a white short-sleeved shirt, scrim scarf, flat cap, high-waisted work trousers with braces, and pit boots. Noticing that the man was out of fashion by several decades, they nudged and whispered to each other. As the man neared, he seemed to turn his head away from them as if trying to avoid eye contact.

In unison they all said, 'Ayup', but there was no answer from the stranger, who blanked them and walked past. A matter of seconds later they turned around and, to their horror, the man had vanished.

Over the years, many motorists have reported seeing the 'Harlington hobo' whilst driving down the road; upon looking through their rear view mirror, he has always disappeared from view.

Harlington village, where the ghost has been seen. (Authors' collection)

eighteen

Hatfield

Hatfield Church

On 10 October 1965, a young man from Doncaster was celebrating his birthday when he decided to take a shortcut through the graveyard. He was in a hurry, not wanting to hang around there on a cold night. Just after turning the corner past the church, he looked up and saw a woman heading towards him, in as much of a hurry as him. He could see quite clearly that she wasn't wearing suitable clothing for such a cold night, just a long dress. He even noticed that whilst his feet were making a crushing noise on the frosty gravel, her footsteps were silent. As the young woman passed him, he turned his head to have another look, and there was no one there – all that remained was a very strong aroma of roses and crushed mint leaves. He cleared the cemetery wall in a single leap and was home in two minutes flat.

nineteen

Hexthorpe

The Silent Signalman

One dark night in late autumn, at the Cherry Tree sidings, a train driver and his second man were looking out through the window of their locomotive, waiting for a signal from the signal guard. After a minute or so, the shunter signalled them with his lamp to proceed down the yard. As the driver turned to open the power controller, he noticed the figure of a man coming across the tracks towards them. He described him as being dressed in a light-coloured mackintosh and cap. He lowered the window and shouted, 'Hey, where do you think you're going?' but the man ignored his question and by this time had reached the line on which the train was travelling. Although the driver could clearly see the man's outline, he couldn't see his face or features, only his cap and a dark mask.

The train passed the man, who was now beyond the driver's view. The driver, turning round to his colleague, said, 'Has that bloke come out clear on your side?'

'No, there's no one here,' was the reply.

Confused at this, they both disembarked the train at opposite sides and proceeded down to the rear of the train to try to find the man. Neither could see any sign of him. By now, the shunter had walked up the siding to where they were standing scratching their heads, and he asked what was wrong. The pair proceeded to tell the shunter what had happened. So the three of them widened the search for the mystery man and looked all around the sidings, but to no avail. There was no sign of anyone. The shunter said that he had heard of the ghost of a man sitting on the buffer stops at the end of the sidings but thought that his mates were trying to frighten him. Now he wasn't so sure.

Several weeks later, the same driver was in the signal box at St James' Junction, which is at the opposite end of Hexthorpe Yard to the previous sighting. He was waiting to conduct a Tinsley train crew into the Decoy marshalling yard at Doncaster. During his conversation with the signalman, he mentioned the ghost. Startled, the signalman told him what had happened the last time he had been on nights in that box.

He had a train and carriages, bound for Wath-on-Dearne, in the section and the

brake van was about twenty yards beyond the signal box. All of a sudden he heard someone shouting. Before he could get to the door of the box, it burst open and in staggered a guard. According to the signalman, the poor fellow was in such a state that he could neither stand nor speak. The signalman sat him down and quickly made him a cup of tea. After a while, the guard was able to tell him what had happened.

The guard said he had been sitting quietly in his brake van, waiting for the train to move off, when the rear door of the van had opened and a man in a light raincoat had walked in without saying a word. The man had then left through the other door without even opening it. The driver knew straightaway that this was the same ghost that he had seen two weeks earlier. Who the ghost was or why he was there no one seems to know, and no further sightings have been reported.

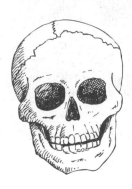

twenty

High Melton

High Melton is a small and quiet place, dominated by its church and nearby hall. Despite the size of the village, it seems to have a high number of residential ghosts

Hauntings of High Melton Hall

The central tower of High Melton Hall is medieval but the main section was built around 1757, with another wing added in 1878. During the Second World War, the hall was used as a prisoner-of-war camp and processed over 3,000 people in total. Although conditions were reasonable, one poor Italian soldier hanged himself the day before being repatriated, after receiving some bad news about his family. In the late 1940s, High Melton Hall was converted into a teacher training college, which it still is today.

High Melton Hall as it stands today. (Authors' collection)

High Melton Hall is a fairly small college and most of the students and teachers know each other, so any new faces get noticed quite quickly. Students have often reported strange people wandering around the corridors at night. When challenged by security, the figures flee back into the darkness and can never be found.

The *Doncaster Chronicle* of 1 July 1954 made the following reference to the hall's ghosts: '… one of the most common sightings is reputed to appear in one of the rooms in the old tower where the walls are so thick that wardrobes and bookshelves have been built into them.'

The most haunted part of the building is arguably the tower, where visitors have been locked in and have had to bang on the doors to get someone's attention. After being released, many have reported that they felt as though they weren't alone in the room; most had also experienced the feeling of panic and a dramatic drop in temperature.

Other unexplained phenomena include: strange smells out of nowhere, cold spots, doors slamming, and voices heard from empty rooms. However, more concerning is the theft of livestock, the remains of which have later been found in the woods.

The Stroller of Hangman Stone Lane

Many years ago, a sixteen-year-old girl was pushing her nine-month-old sibling in a stroller on the steep, winding hill known as Hangman Stone Lane, adjacent to High Melton Hall. Without warning, a horse and carriage came hurtling around the blind

The ghost of a girl with a stroller has been seen here. (Authors' collection)

bend, catching her and the child in its path, and she only had a split second to make a choice; she sacrificed herself by pushing the pram free before going under hoof and cart. Lying at the side of the road, her only concern was for the child and her parents. After hearing that the child was safe, she took her final breath and slipped into the next world.

She is now often seen sitting on the wall at the junction of Hangman Stone Lane and Doncaster Road, awaiting the return of her parents to tell them she's sorry.

The Headless Ghost of High Melton

The junction of Doncaster Road and Hangman Stone Road, at the outskirts of the village, is haunted by a gruesome, headless spectre. It has been described as wearing a dress and blouse and is often thought to be the figure of a woman. Many motorists have at first assumed the figure to be a hitchhiker wanting a lift and have slowed down; however, on drawing near they are alarmed to realise that the torso is drenched in crimson red and the figure has no head.

In the mid-1960s, demolition work was carried out on the old stone farm buildings that once stood at the junction. Workers discovered a skeleton hidden beneath the old stone fireplace hearth. All work on the site stopped and the police were called. A full murder investigation was launched; it wasn't until several weeks later that forensics determined the body to be that of a Celtic warrior dressed in a kilt, who must have died in battle on the site before the building was erected.

Since the discovery of the body, the sightings have become a rare occurrence and it is thought that the reason for his haunting was to draw attention to the scene of his demise. However, it is believed that the haunting will not stop entirely until his head is found.

Site where the headless ghost has been spotted. (Authors' collection)

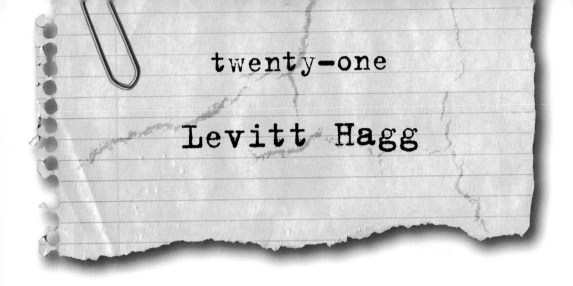

twenty-one

Levitt Hagg

The Hag of Levitt Hagg

Levitt Hagg is now nothing more than a ghost town – the last of its properties were condemned in the 1950s and were demolished around the late 1960s. Legend has it that the village once had its own resident witch – Sally Gooser – who is sometimes credited with being the source of the 'Hagg' part of the town's name. Her name is even thought to be connected with the old nursery rhyme Mother Goose (Mother Goose is often depicted as a witch, flying on her goose familiar).

> Old Mother Goose
> When she wanted to wander
> Would fly through the air
> On a very fine gander.

It is thought that Sally Gooser was the local herbalist who took in sick animals to be cured. However, the locals generally considered her to be a witch and, although they respected her skills, she was shunned by her peers. Parents would tell the village children not to go near Sally's house for fear of them being bewitched. Even long after her death, parents told their children not to go past the house after dark in case Sally Gooser got them. She is said to haunt the deserted town to this very day.

The village as it once was. (Photograph courtesy of Conisbrough & Denaby Main Heritage Group)

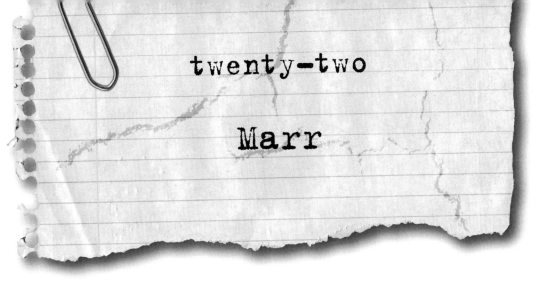

twenty-two

Marr

Hangman Stone Road, Marr

Hangman Stone Road runs from High Melton to Marr, joining at Barnburgh Crags. There are many hauntings associated with this road; here is another, which often gets eclipsed by the better-known Barnburgh legends.

The story goes that, during the reign of Charles II, a sheep stealer was out at midnight undertaking this criminal deed. At the time, sheep stealing was a capital offence. The man had stolen a large ram and tied its four legs together with a strong cord; placing it over his shoulders, he carried it like a rucksack. As he was sneaking homewards in the hours of darkness with his ill-gotten gain, he found the burden rather heavy to bear. When he reached the rock known as Hangman's Stone, he stopped for a rest and placed the sheep on top of a stone to take the weight off his shoulders. However, the sheep began to struggle and fell off the other side, pulling the cord tightly around the man's throat. He tried to free himself and stand up, but the more he tried, the more the sheep kicked and writhed; the longer they fought, the tighter the cord became. In the end, the weight of the sheep strangled the man, who was found dead the next morning, and so the sheep had done the hangman out of a job.

The Ghostly Gallows

One evening, a man was travelling home along Hangman Stone Road heading towards Marr when he witnessed a turn of events which still haunts him today. Here's his story as told to us:

At night, this windy spooky road really gives passers-by the chills. One particular night, many years ago, I was travelling down the road as a passenger – a route I take frequently; looking out across the fields I was amazed to see gallows at the junction of Hangman Stone Lane. Yes, that's right, gallows! I was completely transfixed as we passed by and I just stared in disbelief at what I was seeing.

The gallows were a very tall scaffold frame above a platform and made of what looked like wood, with two pieces of rope on either end of a central cross beam, just swinging in the wind. Obviously the ropes were a noose. The image was as clear as day and although I was shocked, I wasn't scared.

I stared at the gallows until they were out of sight and just sat there in disbelief at what I had witnessed. I never mentioned what I saw even to my friends, until a few years later, knowing that I wouldn't be taken seriously – but I never forgot what I saw that night.

It totally freaked me out but fuelled my belief in the supernatural. It's not like I caught a glimpse. The image lingered on long enough for me to take in all the details. To this day I remember everything about that sighting and ever since on my visits down the road, I look out for the hangman's gallows. But I've never seen them since.

One summer's evening, a family were travelling down Hangman Stone Road after spending the day out, when one of the children said, 'What's that for Daddy? Is it a park?' Slowing down to see what his daughter was referring to, the man glanced across, catching sight of what he describes as a twin gallows made of wood with two rope nooses hanging from a cross bar. Staring in disbelief as they passed by, he thought the gallows must have been placed there for a battle re-enactment or something similar. Curious, he decided to turn the car around and take a closer look. Upon returning up the hill, he pulled into the layby opposite the entrance to Hangman Stone Lane and got out. He walked to where they had seen the gallows, only to discover that the grand structure was no longer there. After searching the internet for information, he came across our website and submitted his strange encounter to us.

Many people believe that Hangman Stone Lane and Hangman Stone Road got their names through the story about the sheep hanging the man, as there were no actual gallows at this site. However, the truth of the matter is that the place takes its name from the stone. The equivalent of today's courts and trials were often held at parish boundary stones, which thus became known as 'Hangman's stones'. These are

Site of the mysterious gallows. (Authors' collection)

found in many counties, which is why the story of the man and sheep has been linked to so many places.

Having visited this area on a number of occasions over the years, we have yet to witness anything for ourselves, but due to the first-hand reports that we have received and the number of other reported sightings of the gallows, their presence seems all too real.

The Miser of Church Lane

Numerous reports have been made of an old man coming out of the graveyard situated on Church Lane. He crosses the road to a small patch of wasteland beside a farm building that used to be the site of an orchard.

A local who has lived in the small hamlet for a number of years had a strange encounter with the old miser. One day, whilst standing at his living room window waiting for a taxi, he saw what he described as a man coming out of the graveyard dressed in Victorian clothing; he wore a long-tailed coat, waistcoat and bowler hat. At first he thought that the man was there for a wedding or funeral, but he soon realised that something was amiss due to the late hour, so he curiously watched. The strange man crossed the road and walked straight through a boundary wall! It was then that the resident remembered the tale he'd heard as a small boy of the old man who buried his savings in the orchard across the road from the church, in the direction of Brodsworth Hall. It is rumoured that the man returns to check his money is still there.

A further sighting of the old miser occurred when an unsuspecting motorist, who was travelling down Church Lane one evening, saw the old man scurry through the church gates and across the road, vanishing before reaching the other side.

It is not known who the man is or if there is any treasure buried nearby, but it just proves that you can't take it with you!

The miser crosses the road here. (Authors' collection)

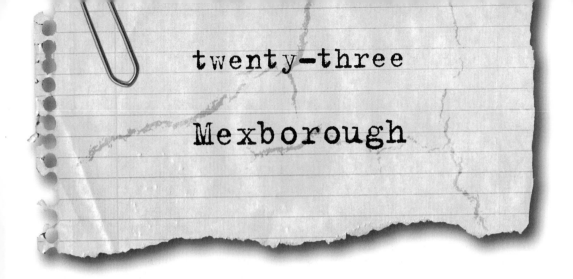

twenty-three

Mexborough

The Ferry Boat Inn

This public house is named after the ferry boat which once carried people across the River Don to Old Denaby. Mrs Walton, an ex-landlady of this establishment, made some discoveries about the building's past whilst looking through old church records. She learnt that during the English Civil War, Royalist Captain Paulden left Pontefract

The Ferry Boat Inn on Ferry Boat Lane. (Authors' collection)

Castle with twenty others in order to capture Cromwellian Rainsborough. Thomas Rainsborough was killed at Doncaster on 29 October 1648. Hostages were taken from Doncaster, and, when they got to the ferry, a skirmish ensued during which a man had his head chopped off outside the building which used to be a rest place for travellers. Later this building became the Ferry Boat Inn.

Over the years, many landlords and landladies have managed the pub. The most common paranormal reports have been the sound of chains rattling and disembodied footsteps, which are heard when the pub is quiet. Numerous sightings have also been reported, by customers and staff alike, of the grey apparition of a Cromwellian soldier pacing up and down the old part of the building, clasped in irons. He is described as being dressed in a metal breastplate over a suede leather coat, wearing bucket-topped riding boots. After seeing the apparition, one of the former landlords used to leave a drink of ale out for the old condemned soldier.

Other sightings have occurred outside the historical pub, where the phantom of a soldier is seen to kneel in a prayer-like position, before his head falls to the floor from decapitation, causing his body to slump to the ground; at this point the head and body disappear from view, leaving the unsuspecting witness wondering what they have seen.

The Haunted Tree

The child mortality rate in Edwardian England was high, with a quarter of children dying before their tenth birthday. These were hard times and, for some, the ritual of séance became the only method of extending their cruelly shortened parenthood.

These séances attempted to entice the spirit of a child into communicating; children's toys were often used as a lure. A Midland toy manufacturer eventually produced a doll specifically designed for séance use. The doll was blessed by the Spiritualist church, and the clay was mixed with salt for purification and to prevent evil entities from interacting with the doll. Between 1882 and 1915, the company produced only forty-two of these melancholic-looking toys for the dead.

In some cases, bereaved parents used a real child, normally female, as a vessel to contact the dead. A séance leader would put the child into a hypnotic state; some believe that this is dangerous, as doing so opens a person up to contact with demonic entities.

A moderately well-off family living in Mexborough at the turn of the twentieth century suffered the loss of their only son – in what they thought was a tragic accident – when he was found hanging from a tree by his school tie. They contacted a celebrated séance leader in the hope of communicating with their deceased child. He was renowned for having a high success rate in contacting dead children by trance mediumship, obtained through the practice of putting his nine-year-old daughter into a hypnotic state.

The séance was arranged to begin at 3 a.m. 'dead time', because the hours between 3 a.m. and 4 a.m. are supposed to be when the veil between the physical world and the spiritual world is at its thinnest. It is often referred to by nurses as the dying time, as that's when most people in hospital pass away. It is also known as the witching hour, and black mass rituals and other dark ceremonies are commonly performed at this time.

A total of five people attended the séance: the deceased child's parents, a family friend, the séance leader and his daughter. The séance began with them all joining hands in a circle, with the séance leader and his daughter seated at opposite ends of the elongated table. The only light was a single candle in the middle of the circle; as it flickered it cast shadows that seemed to dance across the walls, almost as if teasing and taunting the darkness.

The séance leader produced a pocket watch that glistened in the candlelight, and informed the group members that once the state of hypnosis had been reached they

Now a highly sought after antique, séance dolls are renowned for producing unparalleled results. (Authors' collection)

must not break the circle under any circumstances.

'Listen to my voice and only my voice,' he said to his daughter, as he swung the watch in a pendulum motion. 'I will count back from 10; at number 10, you will be standing at the top of a dark staircase; as I count down you will descend down the staircase deeper into the darkness; as I reach number 1 you will be completely in the dark and the only sound you will hear will be my voice.'

He hypnotised his daughter as he had done many times before, then instructed her to venture out into the spirit world to seek out the lost child. 'Use my voice as a guide and venture further into the darkness; find him, find the boy.'

She called out, 'I can't; it's dark in here and it's not the normal place. I think I'm in hell.'

The mother cried, 'Oh no!'

At this, the enraged family friend said, 'Enough is enough!' and demanded that the séance was ended and money refunded. The friend then rose from his seat, breaking the circle. At this, a gust of wind blew through the room, extinguishing the candle and plunging the room into complete darkness. The girl let out an ear-piercing screech. The séance leader stood up and asked the congregation to remain calm, while he fumbled to relight the candle. Once it was lit, they were shocked to discover that the girl had vanished – not just from her seat, but from the locked room.

A search party quickly combed the building from top to bottom in search of the girl, but no trace of her could be found. It was not until daybreak that she was discovered hanging from a nearby tree at the side of the canal, not far from the Ferry Boat Inn. Her father was distraught when he cut down her body, swinging in the morning breeze; he was angered that his daughter had died and blamed the irresponsible behaviour of the family for her tragic death.

Legend says that if you go down to the tree at 3 a.m. you can see the girl hanging, but you can never see the rope she used. People have reported the strange sensation of being strangulated by an unseen force in this area after sunset. Several youngsters who use the area have reportedly seen the girl.

After receiving this story, we didn't think it was anything more than an urban legend, but published a small article on our website regardless…then we received a photograph of what looks like a girl hanging from a tree down by the footpath.

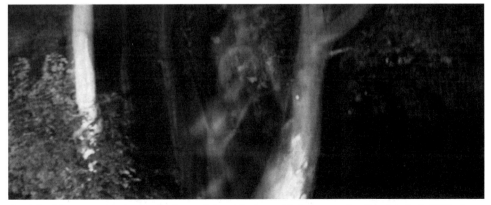

A website visitor sent us this photograph taken on their mobile phone while they were out walking their dog in 2009, after seeing our report of the haunted tree. This picture has not been altered in any way – apart from cropping out the person in the photograph, who did not want to be identified. (Website submission)

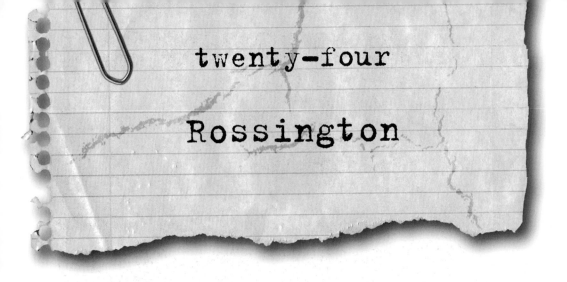

twenty-four

Rossington

The Hauntings of Stripe Road

A couple of spectral women have been reported on Stripe Road in Rossington over the years: one an old hag and one a handsome young woman, apparently from very different eras.

Back in the 1930s, like most mining villages, Rossington boasted a Miners' Welfare Hall and, a couple of nights a week, would host dance nights, attracting the young from the village in droves. In the summer of 1938, four friends had been to the dance and were walking home; it was a warm, clear night, so they decided to take a walk down by the railway line. At that time, the main road that leads over the railway bridge (now Stripe Road) was known as Tickhill Road.

Just as the group approached the bridge, the church bells chimed midnight and they could see what they later described as a 'ghostly girl' sitting on the bridge wall. She was aged around twenty and had a beautiful face. She was wearing a long white dress of a hoop style. They recall that the girl was smiling at them when they passed by, but they felt a cold shiver run through them nonetheless; something about her wasn't quite right. Hurrying down Clay Flat Lane, they turned to discover that the young figure had disappeared, leaving no trace.

Others have reported this handsome young lady, describing her as being dressed in an inappropriate manner, revealing her breasts in a seductive way.

At the top of Stripe Road, near the old farmhouse, there have been sightings of an old and withered lady walking across the street. She is dressed in a grey gown with a hood which is described as being from the early 1600s. The ghostly figure has been seen on several occasions by people from the village, but her identity is unknown.

Rossington Pit Ghost

Like most Yorkshire villages, Rossington was once the home of a successful coal mine, which opened around 1912. Like most mines, lives were lost here – to the count of ninety-two by the time the mine closed in 1986.

One worker reported seeing a miner walking from the weighbridge towards where the bathhouse used to be, before disappearing into thin air. The eyewitness described him as wearing a yellow hat and light, complete with battery pack, and a donkey jacket with NCB written on the back. He also said that the man had coal dust on his face, which blurred any distinguishing features he may have had. The man tried to find the ghostly figure, or rationalise what had just happened, but there was no trace of anyone, living or dead.

Rossington Colliery when it was in use. (Authors' collection)

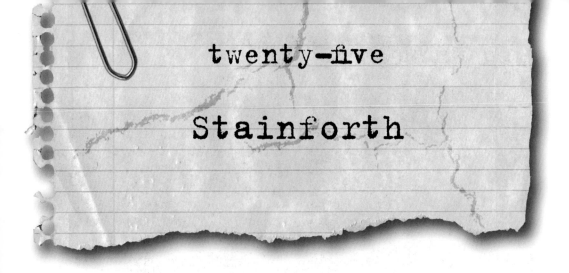

twenty-five

Stainforth

Haggs Wood

This story was submitted to us by a former Boy Scout, 'Russell'.

Russell was nine years old in the 1970s and was camping in the Scout camp near Haggs Wood, just outside Doncaster. The Scouts were out walking and noticed some old ruins in the woods. Boys being boys, they decided to take a closer look, when all of a sudden they heard a voice call, 'Get away from there, it's dangerous!'

Looking up, they noticed an old man walking his dog. Russell describes the man as in his late seventies with a walking stick and flat cap; at his side was his little white Scottie dog. The boys went over to talk to the old man and asked why he considered the ruins dangerous.

Sitting down on a rock, the man began to tell the tale. He started by saying that the old ruins were once the abode of a powerful witch who was well known in the area for her potions and healing remedies, until a spate of infant deaths caused the locals to become convinced that she had cursed them. Then one night they took up arms and burnt her alive inside her house. He

said that, with her dying breath, she pleaded her innocence and vowed to take vengeance, putting a curse upon the villagers' children and stating that she would return and take them with her to hell. Fascinated by the old man's tale, the boys couldn't wait to return to camp and tell of the witch.

The older Boy Scouts were already familiar with the story and took great pleasure in trying to scare the younger ones, adding to the tales of the witch in the woods. Of course, imaginations were running wild and some of the other boys wanted to have a look, so the group set off back to the ruins.

They were all excited and filled with fear. One of the older Scouts stopped short suddenly and was looking around, pointing out noises he heard coming from the woodlands. The place where they had stopped was filled with dead trees, just north of the ruins. They fell silent, listening, trying to hear it. Of course the woods, especially a 'dead' wood area, can make for a lot of strange noises that stir the imagination. They could hear creaks and twigs breaking as if underfoot, which could have been something moving

The creature described by Russell. (Authors' collection)

around: a person, or an animal. But the eldest Scout kept saying 'Can you hear that?' on and on. Russell was not sure if he was just trying to scare them, or if he was really scared himself.

Russell was looking outward through the woods into the distance, squinting his eyes and trying to focus because he kept thinking he could see something, but would then lose sight of it. He then real-ised what he was looking at, and could feel it watching him as if its stare was piercing him with daggers.

It was dreadful. What he saw seemed to be an old woman, but she looked like she was part of the woodlands. Her face looked like it was made from stone cov-ered in moss – masking it, making it look like part of its surroundings. Her hair was made of silver and grey birch twigs, her hands of roots, the eyes, he could see clearly, were like two black holes pull-ing him in. The mouth was filled with teeth made of razor-sharp thorns, and, as he stared, frozen to the spot with fear, he kept seeing it move, fast, like some ravaged beast scouring through the woods stalking its prey.

Mesmerised, he slipped head-first down the banking, hitting his head on a large stone. The rest of the Scouts ran to his aid in a panic at the sight of the blood spew-ing from the gash on his head, but all they could get out of Russell was, 'The Witch; the Witch; it's coming for us!'

He claimed to see it a few times whilst being helped back to camp, but could not fully make it out, as it seemed to be cam-ouflaging itself to the woods, running from tree to tree. The troop leader took him to Doncaster Royal Infirmary, where they stitched him up and sent him back to camp, but things were weird after the accident. All Scouts were confined to the camp after one of the tents was found with claw marks ripped in the side of it; even the adults were acting strangely after that.

Even today the stories circulate amongst the Scouts about the old hag of Haggs Wood.

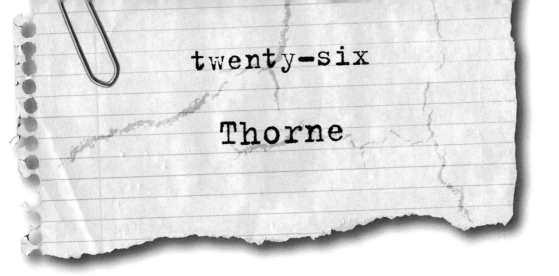

twenty-six

Thorne

The Punch Bowl

This quaint hotel is reported to have accommodated some guests who checked out but have never left. The property was originally built by the local mine owner as a deputy's house. Over the years, it has been extended and renovated to the fine splendour of today; it is now an independent hotel owned by the Old Mill Brewery.

Many sightings of a small spectral boy have been reported; he likes to engage in playful antics with unsuspecting guests. Staff have also reported the feeling of being watched in the cellar and some have even been tapped on their shoulders. The most intriguing haunting, though, is in Room 12, where many guests have had the feeling of being held down on the bed by a strange force.

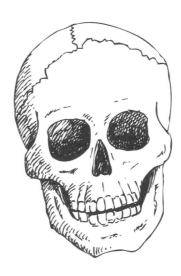

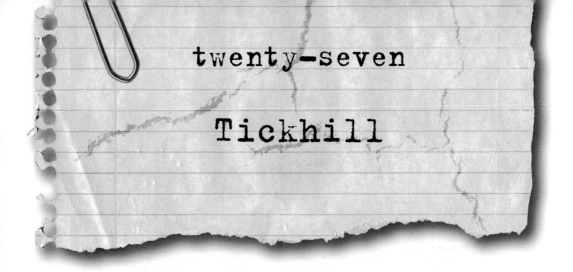

twenty-seven

Tickhill

Wong Lane

The historic Doncaster village of Tickhill, resplendent with its own twelfth-century castle, is reached via equally ancient stretches of road which cut through the fields surrounding it. It is more than likely that some of these roads were once medieval trade routes, which were improved in the last two centuries for regular use by coach and horses.

The following story concerns one such road, known as Wong Lane. On a crystal clear, cold winter's evening in the mid-1960s, a man was driving along Wong Lane, returning home after performing as a musician at a late dance in Doncaster. In the distance, travelling along the rail-

way embankment, he saw what appeared to be the silhouette of an old-fashioned railway carriage with dimly lit windows. Surprised at its antiquated shape, and indeed the lack of any engine sound, the man looked more closely. He was amazed to see that the silent vehicle illuminated by the moonlight was not a railway carriage at all, but a stagecoach pulled by black horses. The coach disappeared from vision behind a large tree ... and did not reappear on the other side.

On returning home, the man told his wife of his strange experience. For almost twenty years, neither of them thought any more about it – until two friends of his wife told how they too had seen a phantom stagecoach travelling along

Location where the death coach is sometimes seen. (Authors' collection)

The death coach.

The Millstone public house. (Authors' collection)

Wong Lane one moonlit night, before it vanished into thin air.

This ghostly coach has been observed on numerous occasions, dashing down Wong Lane before fading from view. Also, strange figures from other times have been seen walking along the roadside; perhaps these apparitions have caused some of the road accidents along that particular road.

In folklore, death travelled in a pitch-black horse-drawn coach. People who have reported such sightings of a coach and horse have sometimes claimed that the driver had no head. The 'death coach' passes at midnight and makes no sound. It is said to be a harbinger of death, and once it has come to earth it cannot return empty

The Millstone Public House

The Millstone, on the corner of Westgate and Dam Road, takes its name from the nearby medieval Tickhill Mill. According to staff and customers, a ghostly Lady in Black, carrying a scythe, walks through walls and stands by tables. It is not known who the mystery lady is, but she certainly gives the unsuspecting patrons a fright.

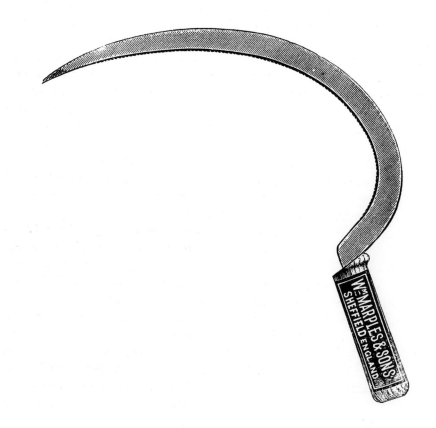

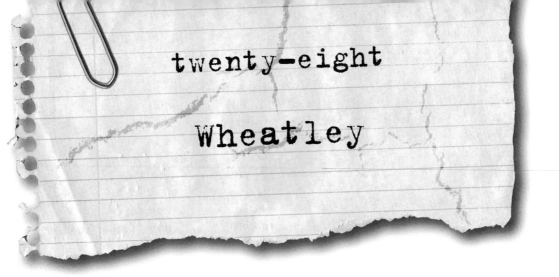

Witch of Wells Road

Wells Road has been the centre of reported malevolent poltergeist activity. Interestingly, the street is built on the site of three wells that once served Wheatley Hall. It is also said to have been the site of local witch trials centuries ago – and suspected witches were once cast down these wells.

From the fifteenth century to the late-eighteenth century, a wave of persecution washed across Europe. Most of those accused of witchcraft were women, and it was generally older women and those of the poorer classes who suffered most. Women who worked in the areas of healing, midwifery and cookery were most likely to be accused of making spells, potions and poisons. However, anyone who posed a threat to either the Church or the Crown was likely to be accused too. Any crop failure, famine or disease could be attributed to the 'Evil Eye', and a scapegoat would be quickly found; normally, a widowed woman would suffice.

Joan Jurdie of Rossington, Doncaster, was accused of witchcraft in 1605; the depositions of several of her neighbours were taken before Hugh Childers, the Mayor of Doncaster. We take the accusations levelled against her from this account.

It seems that Joan was requested to assist the birth of Peter Mirfin's wife Jennet – but Joan was found guilty of the unpardonable slight of not attending until four or five days after the important event was over. This neglect was allegedly because Jennet had previously spurned her hospitality and had later declined to partake of the cake or refreshments offered by Joan.

When his wife took a turn for the worse after Joan's visit, Mr Mirfin suspected that a curse had been placed upon his house. Further suspicion was aroused when his wife died shortly afterwards. Witnesses of Joan's occult practices were then called for. One neighbour testified that Joan had said Peter Mirfin and his wife 'had better have come and partaken of her hospitality'. To others, Joan had supposedly claimed that Mrs Mirfin would 'be worse before she was better'.

Prior to her death, the sick woman herself, Jennet Mirfin, had declared that she was 'witch-ridden'; when asked to explain her condition, she replied, 'Never worse; weak, very weak, Woe worth her! She hath kill'd me; I may never recover.' On being asked to whom she alluded, she exclaimed, 'I was well until Joan Jurdie came.' Two days later she had died – according to her husband, 'growing sick immediately after her milk turned into blood'.

The whole village was now up in arms against Joan. Joan had allegedly been heard to say that she would get even with William Dolfin and William Wainwright, 'for what they had said against her' after the death of Mrs Mirfin. William Dolfin's wife bore testimony that, six years before, she had sought the help of Joan for her sick child, and that she knew a woman who had also sought her help for a sick calf. She was induced to suspect that Joan Jurdie was a witch 'because she doth take upon her to help such things'.

Within fourteen days of this statement, several animals belonging to William Dolfin fell sick, even though there was no outbreak of sickness in the village. Joan Jurdie had to appear a second time before Hugh Childers and other justices to answer for her further deeds of darkness. She, however, deposed before these dignitaries of the law that she had no skill to help sick folk, or cattle, nor had she ever taken it upon herself to meddle with any such matter. She denied saying to Dolfin's wife that she would get even with her and her husband; she also denied saying that Peter Mirfin's wife would be worse before she was better. The outcome of her trial is unknown, but one suspects it was not favourable.

Suspected witches and heretics would have faced 'trial by water', being tossed into the water to see if they would float. If they floated, they were deemed witches and would be hanged in the lynch fields. Could this now be the site of Lichfield Road? If they sank, they were considered innocent – but their fate was already sealed.

The case of Joan Jurdie is the only documented case that we could find, but that doesn't mean there weren't more witch trials here. Could Joan, or others who were accused and executed for the crime of witchcraft, be responsible for the poltergeist activity in the area?

The Wells Road Hauntings

A former resident of Wells Road contacted us to share her account of living in one of the properties. During her time there, she had experienced a number of apparitions and extreme poltergeist activity.

It all started on the very first day she moved in, back in 1981, when one of her neighbours informed her that the previous occupants had been forced to get a priest in to exorcise the property after being terrorised by the ghost of an old witch. This had eventually led to them moving. Not being a believer, the woman dismissed this warning and moved in regardless; however, unnerving events soon began to unfold.

In the first week, whilst she was watching television, just about to go to bed, a family portrait that hung over the fireplace suddenly levitated about a foot from the wall before hurtling into the middle of the sitting room floor, smashing at her feet. Startled, she stood up in disbelief and started to clear away the debris. Her mind cast back to her brother and sister, who had been killed in a road accident in 1980.

She thought perhaps it was them trying to pass on a message, and, taking comfort from this, she pushed the incident to the back of her mind.

As time went by, the paranormal activity got stranger by the day. Things would go missing and then reappear in odd places – a knife in the washing machine and keys in the fridge; strange, perhaps, but not totally unexplainable. Then a smell like rotten eggs or sulphur was noticed, but on investigation by council officials no cause could be found.

One evening, while the woman's husband was working away, the activity increased. Just before heading up to bed, she locked the doors and turned out the lights before checking on her children. She'd been asleep for around half an hour when she was woken by music blaring out at full blast. Jumping out of bed, confused and running on adrenalin, she fled downstairs only to find that all the lights were back on and the record player was playing at full volume! Turning it off, she stood still and listened for an intruder; her heart was pounding. She went to the kitchen and got a large knife to defend herself, before checking that all the doors and windows were locked. Perplexed, she wondered if one of her children was sleepwalking. Was she going mad? She just didn't know! That night she slept in the children's room, too scared to be alone. However, things didn't seem too bad in the cold light of day and she convinced herself that it must have been a power surge.

The following evening, she'd forgotten all about the night before and was relaxing on the settee when a little boy walked into the room. For a second she thought it was her own son, but soon realised it wasn't and challenged the boy, surmising that he was from next door or lost. But he just stood there, staring around the room. She describes him as having big brown eyes, a 1950s'-style haircut and wearing old-fashioned stripy blue and white pyjamas. She asked again if he was ok and, receiving no reply, she reached out to touch his shoulder – but as she did so he vanished. 'What! Was that a ghost?' she thought – but he was so clear, and as large as life. 'Bless him,' she thought, 'it's just a poor little boy lost and alone.'

But things didn't stop there, and he wasn't alone! She'd often return home to find that mirrors were turned to face the walls and pictures had fallen down; lights would go on and off of their own accord; a crucifix that hung in the hallway would turn itself upside down; her Jack Russell dog would never settle and would bark at things that weren't there; and, on one occasion, the door under the stairs slowly opened, almost as if someone or something was watching her from the shadows. As she edged her way closer to peer into the darkness, the door slammed shut in her face, leaving a foul stench of sulphur.

One evening, after she had turned off her bedside lamp to go to sleep, she heard footsteps in the hallway outside her room; opening one eye, she half expected to see her little boy or girl come running in, but nothing. Then there was a creaking noise, as if they were standing behind the door. She sat up in bed and waited; still nothing.

'Hello? I know you're there, come in,' she called. Still nothing. Then the door slowly started to creak open – just a few inches at first, then a little more; by the time the door was open a foot wide, the woman was sat at the foot of her bed waiting to comfort her children, but still they delayed. When the door was finally fully open, she saw something standing in the doorway. The figure was hazy, smoky, hard to make out. Something was wrong, very wrong! Her eyes darted from side to side, scanning the figure that slowly materialised until she could see the full face unfold out of the darkness. It was contorted and twisted: an old woman's face. The lips were blackened and withered, and putrid black pus trickled from the corner of its mouth. The hair was long and grey, but its eyes were bright blue – as bright as sapphires; piercing beady blue eyes that burned right into her soul. While their eyes were locked in this supernatural duel, the rest of its body continued to form. It was obscure but she could see that it was wearing an old, worn-out black dress, dripping wet. She refused to yield to its piercing glare; it gnarled its face in disgust, turning its head before folding itself back into the dark mist, slowly disappearing, leaving nothing but the sour stench of death.

She was so scared by this encounter that she gathered her children and hurried to a friend's house – and didn't go home until the weekend, when her husband returned from work. Exasperated at her claims that she was seeing ghosts, he found it hard to swallow, but, seeing his wife so upset, he took a week off work. Things soon settled down and he returned to work. However, not long after this, their seven-year-old daughter started to have trouble sleeping and wanted to stay in her mother's bed. Mother and child found solace in this arrangement until the weekend, when the woman's husband returned home.

It was late, around 3 a.m., when an ear-splitting scream shattered the dead silence of the night. Both parents flew out of bed and raced to their little girl's room. She was still screaming as they burst through the door – just in time to catch a glimpse of a black wisp of smoke dispersing above the bed.

'What's wrong?' cried her mother.

The little girl screamed, 'The old lady wouldn't let me sleep!'

'What old lady?' asked her mother.

'The old lady with black lips and bright blue eyes who was floating over my bed; you must have seen her, she was right there.' The parents quickly exchanged a glance and took the girl to their bed for the rest of the night.

The next day, an argument ensued about the previous night. 'You shouldn't put such nonsense in her head. First you were saying there's a little boy and then you start going on about a witch! Now she's seeing it! And you wonder why?' said the woman's husband, slamming the door on his way to work. However, he phoned home at dinnertime with an excited tone in his voice: 'I've sorted it out … I'll prove there are no ghosts.'

'What do you mean?' she asked him.

'I've got a Ouija board – I'll show you there's no such thing.'

Reluctantly the woman agreed; she wasn't sure what was worse, the arguing or the hauntings.

Sending the kids to her mum's, they set the board up on the coffee table. Placing their fingers on the glass, in unison they took a breath.

'Is there anyone who wants to talk to us?' he asked. 'Is there anyone there? … See? Nothing!' he said.

But then the glass slowly started to move around the board; very slowly, it spelled out Y…E…S… Their eyes widened.

'Stop pushing it,' she said.

'I'm not! Who's there? What do you want?' he asked.

It started spelling out words – not in English, but an older language. Some words they still understood: diabolus… spiritus… witches…

'Get out and leave us alone!' the husband shouted. The woman took her hand off the glass but it continued to move, only now faster, until the man could no longer hold on to it. It continued to spin and dance around the table until the glass and light bulb above exploded simultaneously, plunging them into darkness and showering them both with jagged shards of glass. They ran out into the street, holding each other close.

'It's ok. It's ok. We don't have to go back,' the woman's husband said, squeezing his wife tightly.

It was only after reading our appeal for information on Wells Road that the woman understood what might have been the cause of her hauntings!

Other poltergeist activity has been reported in this area and several properties have now been demolished. After contacting Doncaster Council, we were informed that they didn't hold any records of supernatural events; however, the same request was made to South Yorkshire police, who did confirm that they had received a number of 999 calls regarding paranormal activity in Wheatley, but could neither confirm nor deny that they were from Wells Road.

Sayers Tyres

Sayers Tyres, on Athron Street, is on the site of a former chapel that served as a makeshift mortuary during the Second World War. Over the years it has been plagued by paranormal activity, including visitations of a spectre that witnesses have described as wearing 1940s'-style clothing.

Reports from garage workers date back to the early 1990s, when tyres started mysteriously moving around. Puzzled by this, the owner used to mentally note where things were before he left of an evening; upon arriving the following morning, things had often moved – such as tyres being stacked where they previously hadn't been. In addition to this, small objects were thrown at staff and customers.

The owner at the time was so terrified that he had the building exorcised in an attempt to stop the unearthly happenings. Things got progressively stranger in 2003 when coins mysteriously appeared, as though they had fallen from the roof. Then one night, as the owner was locking the doors for the evening, he heard an almighty crash from within the building. Opening the doors to see what had happened, he was shocked to see that two lead weights, which were used to balance tyres, had projected towards the door, causing the noise he had heard.

Shortly afterwards, the owner sold up and left; the ghostly happenings seemed to stop for a while – until 2007, when things started to happen again.

The new owner was sceptical about the stories until he started to find old coins on the garage floor, dating back to before the war. The first he found was an old penny piece, dated 1936 and bearing the image of George VI. Then a second coin, dated 1938, was lying in almost the same spot several weeks later.

Various newspapers have run this story throughout the last decade, including the *Daily Mail*. It is unknown who the spectral figure is, as countless souls must have passed through the building when it was used as a mortuary.

twenty-nine

Some Additional Hauntings

Whilst researching this book, we found that Doncaster has indeed played host to a high level of strange phenomena throughout the years. And, even to this day, people are reporting such occurrences to the authorities. We sent out Freedom of Information requests to South Yorkshire police, Doncaster Council and Doncaster NHS trust, requesting any information that they held on file. Doncaster Council and Doncaster NHS claimed not to hold information on paranormal incidents. However, South Yorkshire police did state that they held such records, which included three accounts of poltergeist activity that had been reported to them from the Finningley, Thorne and Wheatley areas of Doncaster.

Between June 2006 and June 2011, a total of 597 incidents of a paranormal kind were recorded. However, due to costs and time scales we were unable to gain individual details on each case. During our quest to find the stories and information for this book, we were contacted by a few people who had made such reports. Due to the sensitive nature of these, we were asked not to disclose names and locations, but below is a brief outline of what we received.

Private House in Bentley

A report was made by the occupier that the figure of an old woman had appeared on the stairs and pushed her unsuspecting victim down them. His research showed that an old lady had once lived in the property and had been burgled; during the struggle, she had stumbled to her death on the same stairs.

Marshgate

There's an old warehouse where figures of ghosts are seen on the top floors, peering through the windows. These are rumoured to be people who have disappeared without a trace. Also in this area, reports have been made of a time slip, where people have walked back in time to the Edwardian era.

Creepy Hollow

Near Skellow in Doncaster is a wood that's locally named Creepy Hollow. Many reports have been made to police after cars have broken down for no reason at a junction near the wood. The unsuspecting drivers claim that the car gets surrounded by an unknown dark entity, which attacks several times before disappearing back into the trees.

Could Doncaster be the most haunted place in England?

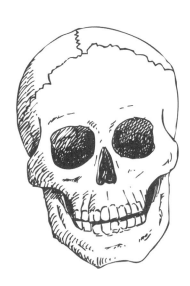

If you enjoyed this book, you may also be interested in...

Haunted Rotherham

RICHARD BRAMALL & JOE COLLINS

This fascinating book contains a terrifying collection of true-life tales from in and around Rotherham. Featuring stories such as the Lunatic of Ulley Reservoir and the Old Hag of Hellaby Hall, this pulse-raising compilation of unexplained phenomena, apparitions, poltergeists, curses, spirits and boggards will delight everyone interested in the paranormal.

978 0 7524 6117 5

Haunted Yorkshire Dales

SUMMER STREVENS

Discover the darker side of the Dales with this terrifying collection of true-life tales from across the region. Featuring chapters on ecclesiastic ectoplasms, ghostly creatures, Ladies in Black and star-crossed spooks, this book will captivate locals and visitors alike.

978 0 7524 5887 8

Haunted Scarborough

MARK RILEY

A fascinating collection of spine-chilling tales from around Scarborough. From poltergeists and mummies to the Headless Man and the mysterious story of the vanishing houses, this book includes many pulse-raising narratives that are guaranteed to make you blood run cold.

978 0 7524 5442 9

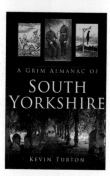

A Grim Almanac of South Yorkshire

KEVIN TURTON

A Grim Almanac of South Yorkshire is a collection of stories from the county's past – some bizarre, some fascinating, some macabre, but all equally absorbing. Revealed here are the dark corners of the county, where witches, body snatchers, highwaymen and murderers, in whatever guise, have stalked. Accompanying this cast of gruesome characters are old superstitions, omens, strange beliefs and long-forgotten remedies for all manner of ailments.

978 0 7524 5678 2

Visit our website and discover thousands of other History Press books.

www.thehistorypress.co.uk